Lr 7

D1405123

DATE DUE

Webb			
APRIL - 1 - 01			
W.M.	4/04		
E.H. 5P			
Hatfield M			
M 01			
W Fleming	6/02		
J.C.	2-10-04		
K. Lile	3-24-0		
D. Jenkins			
	09		
W M			
GAYLORD			PRINTED IN U.S.A.

Renegade Army

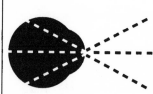

This Large Print Book carries the
Seal of Approval of N.A.V.H.

Renegade Army

Chet Cunningham

hm 5102
21 95
12-00

Thorndike Press • **Thorndike, Maine**

Copyright© 1988 by Chet Cunningham/BookCrafters

All rights reserved.

Published in Large Print in 2000 by arrangement with
Chet Cunningham.

Thorndike Press Large Print Western Series.

The tree indicium is a trademark of Thorndike Press.

The text of this Large Print edition is unabridged.
Other aspects of the book may vary from the original edition.

Set in 16 pt. Plantin by Al Chase.

Printed in the United States on permanent paper.

Library of Congress Cataloging-in-Publication Data
Cunningham, Chet.
    Renegade army / Chet Cunningham.
        p.   cm. — (Pony soldiers #8)
    ISBN 0-7862-2982-9 (lg. print : hc : alk. paper)
    1. Soldiers — Fiction.   2. Indian agents — Fiction.
    3. Large type books.   I. Title.
    PS3553.U468 R46 2000
    813′.54—dc21   00-064791

Renegade Army

1

Short Knife laughed as the white man tried to defend himself with a pitchfork. The man was taller than Short Knife by half-a-foot, had wide shoulders and strong arms, but he was clumsy. He tried to lunge while holding the fork ready.

The Comanche waited for the obvious move when the white-eye paused to recover his balance. Then Short Knife jumped forward, changed directions as the white man reacted, and slashed with his knife across the rancher's unprotected face.

His knife sank in a quarter-of-an-inch, cut through the cheek into his mouth and grated on bone. The rancher screamed and swung around with the pitchfork.

There was no more time to play, no time to torture the rancher. Short Knife lifted the old Griswold and Gunnison revolver and shot the white-eye in the chest.

The rancher jolted backward as if he had been kicked by a war pony as the heavy .44 caliber round from the former Confederate pistol tore into his chest, splintered two ribs, then plunged through his heart and killed him immediately.

Short Knife stepped forward quickly, searched the roundeye's trouser pockets and found a purse. He tied it to his surcingle and then ran for the house. It had not been set on fire yet.

Inside the four room house, three Comanches tore up the place looking for loot. They were more selective now about what they took. Agent Saterlee didn't like them bringing back things that could be identified.

One of the warriors threw aside a leather pouch that clanked when it hit the floor. Short Knife kicked it aside, then when no one watched him, he picked it up and tied it to his surcingle. He knew what was in it. There was nothing left in the house they could use.

The five warriors rapidly loaded a sack of beans and two other gunny sacks filled with food on one of the war ponies and tied everything down. Then they fired the house.

A woman in her thirties and a girl about fifteen lay on the ground outside where they had been violated. They were naked, raped and dead.

Short Knife let his face split with a grin. It had been a good raid. They would eat up the evidence before any of the reservation police could find it.

He opened the leather pouch from his belt and his eyes shone. Inside were six gold double eagles! Over a hundred of the white man's dollars! Short Knife was Comanche but unlike all but one or two on the reservation, he knew the value of the white-eye's coins and paper money. He had spent two years at a Texas mission school when he was fourteen and had quickly learned to speak, read and write English, to wear white man's clothes and understand how stupid and weak the white men were.

The five Comanches raced away from the burning Texas ranch with whoops of delight. They took the ranch's only two horses and drove six head of Texas Longhorns ahead of them. The beef would give them some solid food again. The animals would be kept in the secret place where their outlawed horses were also hidden. The beef could be slaughtered as they needed it. There was no use in sharing such a bounty with the others on the reservation.

With the gold Short Knife knew he could buy many things. A good rifle, ammunition, blankets, even beef when he couldn't steal it. Gold! He had never seen so much. It was a small fortune. Many white-eyes worked half a year for that much money. He checked the purse he had found on the rancher.

It contained four paper bills, a one, two fives and a ten. Another twenty-one dollars! He was the richest Indian in the Comanche nation! He rode on with a smile. It was a good day to be alive!

Short Knife was tall for a Comanche at 5'8". He had long black hair tied back with a band of beaded elk hide. His nose was firm and strong between deep set black eyes. His left cheek held an old scar from where an arrow had sliced into him. His left hand's third finger was gone from a bravery rite. He was the son of a chief, now dead, and had hopes of becoming a chief before he was lost on a raid and given two years of the white-eye's education poison.

They drove the stock as fast as was practical. At this pace they would be back at their reservation early the next morning, before it grew light. The land the great white father had given them stood at the very eastern end of the panhandle of the Indian Territories. They were less than two miles from the Kansas border and about forty miles from the Texas panhandle. For Short Knife and his four men it was a perfect location for raiding. The Kansas authorities paid little attention to raids into Texas.

The Texas people were too far away to be effective in chasing them or controlling the area.

Short Knife rode with his men, moving at the animals' pace, driving the stubborn steers through the heat of the day. They would soon cross the shallow Kiowa River and the animals could drink their fill.

It had been a good raid, short, and had provided enough food to feed their five families for several weeks whether the Agency food arrived on time or not.

Short Knife smiled. He had a good arrangement with Agent Hirum Saterlee. He helped out the Agent when he had some of his "special work" to do, and in return the Agent looked the other way when Short Knife and his specialists rode south to Texas to raid the small ranchers and settlers scattered through the panhandle.

Yes, it was a fine relationship!

Slade Rogers sat in the worst of the four bars in Prairie City, Kansas. The small excuse for a town had no more than 500 people and owed its existence to half-a-dozen fair-sized cattle ranches and a few dozen sodbusters close by along the Cimarron River. Four years ago, the small town had withered to less than a hundred souls after a bad cattle year, but now it had regenerated itself.

Some said that Fort Larson, about a mile downstream on the river near the line into the Indian Territories, was what brought the town back. Fort Larson had been built two years ago as the major army resupply point for the off-the-railroad line army operations in that area of Kansas, Texas and the Territories.

Slade slammed his beer mug back on the wooden counter and glared at the barkeep. Slade stood tall and thin against the bar. He was 36 years old, six-one, with an uncombed mass of brown hair falling over his ears and collar. He hadn't had a haircut or shave in a year. He had an unkempt, dirty, full beard. From this mass of hair stared soft blue eyes and a small nose that almost vanished in his moustache.

"Another beer!" Slade demanded. The apron held out his hand, took the mug and then held it out again for the nickel. He knew his customers. Sometimes Slade had the money, sometimes he didn't.

"Hell, I drink too much," Slade said hoisting the cold beer. At least there was still ice in the ice house. He talked to himself in the small mirror in back of the bar. The terrible pain came again in the back of his head. He tried to talk over it, to think through the knifing agony of the pain.

"Sure I drink too much. What the hell else I got to do? Work all day at the hardware store, have supper at Molly's and come over here and drink."

Slade grinned. " 'Cept for last night!" He looked around, and this time watched the apron. "Last night I done killed myself three Indians! Comanche, Kiowa maybe. Not sure. Got me three of them bastards!"

"Sure you did, Slade," the apron said. "You got three of them."

"Did so!" The pain seemed to grow into a white hot poker that fried his brain as it dug deeper and deeper. He cupped his hands over his ears for a moment, then shook his head to clear it.

"Did so! Got me two with my pistol and then this third one jumped up with a knife and a club so I kicked the little fucker to death!" Slade's eyes were wide, his breath coming quickly. He looked around again. "Hey, barkeep, don't you go telling nobody 'bout what I said."

"Hell, no," the man behind the bar said quickly. "Won't tell no one, Slade. You know me."

Slade finished the new beer, belched and looked at the back of the bar. "Got to see where you moved the pisser," he said and wandered out the back door.

A man in a black suit at the end of the bar frowned at the apron.

"Slade there. Was he joking about killing three Indians?"

"Slade don't joke any more. He used to. Near a year ago some renegades got to his little farm down on the Cimarron. He'd come into town for supplies and them savages done awful to his wife and two kids. Just done them terrible. They killed them all but the bastards done it slow, Injun slow. Damn hard way to die when a Comanche has the time.

"Old Slade just about lost his mind. He bought three rifles and six pistols and three or four fighting knifes and went looking for Indians. Sheriff brought him back once when he charged into the reservation.

"Since then he's been working in the hardware store. Lives in the back of the store in a room the owner, O'Reilly, built for him. Now Slade works and drinks and then he dreams of killing Indians."

"Poor man," the agent in the black suit said. He tossed the barkeep a quarter. "Set him up to five beers when he comes back," the gent said and went out the front door.

Slade Rogers was not as drunk as he

seemed when he weaved out the back door of the saloon. He used the two-holer, then straightened and checked the pistol at his waist. The beer had done nothing to dull the pain in the back of his head. He was ready. Slade ran half a block down the alley, then another half block along First Street. A horse stood tied at the rail in front of Welton Jones' saddle shop.

Slade pulled the tie reins, mounted, and rode off to the south. He would be on the reservation in twenty minutes.

Prairie City had been built south of the Cimarron River where it swung north for a short ways into Kansas. Slade soon crossed the boundary line between Kansas and the Indian Territories and turned slightly west to the spot he wanted. The Cimarron Kiowa–Comanche Agency lands were larger than some and had various bands and tribes scattered. This was fine with Slade. He came toward three tipis in the darkness and watched. There was no movement.

Then he heard singing, drunken singing, and three bucks came out of one tipi. As they lifted the flap a yellow triangle of light slashed into the night, then at once the light vanished. The three Kiowas stood sharing the same bottle as they talked and laughed.

Slade understood none of what was said,

but he knew the situation. Drunk Indians were easy Indians. He took out the knife he always carried. It was six inches long, a skinning knife. He had used it often on his farm. For a moment he had to squeeze his pale blues eyes shut tightly to try to ward off the pain.

When his eyes were shut, the horror of finding his family came back. The farm buildings had been a blazing, smoking ruin when he rode up after galloping the last terrible mile. His wife lay spreadeagled on the dirt, hands and feet tied to stakes driven into the ground. She was naked, violated, not moving.

Slade saw again the vicious red slices on her white body. Each had bled so he knew they had been made while she was alive. The damned savages had cut her after raping her, to torture her so she would die slowly. Three slices had been made on each side of both breasts. Her nipples had been cut off.

More cuts down her sides, across her stomach and down her soft, sensitive inner thighs. God how she must have suffered!

Slade slammed his fist into the ground where he knelt in the Indian Nations reservation. The sound brought him back to the present. He looked at the Indians. They finished the liquor and one threw the bottle into the brush near the river.

They all laughed again and one turned, evidently heading for his tipi to the left. He staggered and stumbled and laughed as he walked. He wore pants like a white man, but no shirt. A necklace of beads and a single feather in his hair completed his attire.

Slade moved with the lone red man, taking care not to break any twigs or sticks as his feet came down gently on the stretch of land near the river.

The Indian stopped to urinate. Slade looked back the way they had come. Only twenty yards separated them from the place the three Comanches had been talking. The other two were nowhere in sight.

Slade lifted his knife and ran lightly forward, the skinning knife held in front of him like a lance. At the last moment the red man must have sensed more than heard someone near. He started to turn.

The slender blade drove into the Indian's side, penetrated the bottom of his lung and sliced two vital arteries below the heart in half. The Comanche brave's eyes went wide as he completed the turn and stared at Slade for just a moment.

Then his arms swung out as if reaching for Slade as he fell forward, his face digging a short furrow in the dirt as he came to rest.

Slade had jerked the long thin knife from the body as it fell. He knew there would be no need for a second thrust. For a moment he stood there hating the dead Indian. Then deliberately he cut the man's ears off, then his nose. As a final indignity to the red man, Slade scalped him and threw the bloody hair into the river for it to float downstream.

Slade stared at the red man a moment more, then felt his anger fade. The bloody pictures of Julie in his mind receded and slowly dissolved. He shook his head, wiped the blood off his blade on the dead Indian's pants and silently walked back to where he had left his horse a mile to the north.

The pain was gone now, that terrible pain that came in the back of his head and wouldn't go away. He had found only one way to make the pain stop. One way. He looked at his hands. They had streaks of blood on them. Slade smiled. That was how he killed the pain. Each time he killed an Indian he could kill a little more of the terrible pain.

Fourteen. He figured it would take at least fifty of the small red men to equal one white woman, then another fifty for each of his children. He had the time, there were plenty of Indians. He knew that the pain would soon come again.

Lieutenant Colonel Colt Harding came through the gate at Fort Larson and stopped a moment. What a difference from the palisaded, fully secure feeling at Fort Phil Kearny in Wyoming! This was a plains army post — nothing more than a collection of wooden buildings assembled around a roughly rectangular parade ground.

To Colt Harding, a fort was a fort. He had been sent here by General Phil Sheridan to do a specific job, and he would do it regardless of what the place looked like.

He kicked his mount toward a single story frame building near the flag pole. The building had a lettered sign over the door: "Fort Larson Supply Depot, Kansas."

A sentry ran out, saluted and took Colt's horse.

"Colonel Mason's office, trooper?"

"Yes, sir, this is it. Right inside."

Colt stood for a minute looking around the fort. He was glad to get out of the saddle. Colt Harding was six-two and a trim 185 pounds. He wore his brown hair shortly cropped and now had a thick, full moustache. His face was wind and sun burned from many days and nights in the field.

His permanent rank was major, but he had been breveted a light colonel for "special duties," and reported directly to General Phil Sheridan. He turned now and with that rolling gait so common to men who spend a lot of time in the saddle, went up the steps and into the post headquarters.

He had given them time to know he was coming. A master sergeant greeted him at the door.

"Good morning, sir, and welcome to Fort Larson."

"Thank you, Sergeant. Colonel Mason, is he in?"

A figure stepped into an open door and nodded. The bird colonel was not smiling.

"Been waiting for you all morning. What's Phil got up his sleeve this time to bedevil me?"

"Not a blessed thing, Colonel. Can we talk?"

The Fort Commander lost a little of his frown as he waved Colt into his office and shut the door.

Colt did it by the book.

"Lieutenant Colonel Colt Harding, reporting to the Fort Commander as ordered."

Colonel Mason lost some of his reserve.

"Yeah, yeah. I got a copy of your orders two days ago. I can't make a jackass for breakfast out of the blasted paper. What in hell does it mean?"

Colt laughed. "Colonel, that's exactly what we hoped that the Department of the Interior and the Bureau of Indian Affairs would think. More army doubletalk. I'll be glad to explain."

"About damn time." Colonel Mason opened a box on his desk. "Want a cigar? Get these from Atlanta. Damn good even if they are rebel made."

Colt took the offered stogie, unwrapped it, bit off the end tip and lit it with a match from a small box the colonel pushed toward him.

Both men sat down and Colt blew a mouthful of smoke at the exposed rafters of the ceiling.

"General Sheridan isn't happy with what's been going on at the Indian Agency here, the Cimarron Kiowa–Comanche. From what he can find out, the place seems to be functioning as a safe zone for bunches of Comanches who have been raiding all over northern Texas."

"Nothing new about that."

"It seems to be worse than usual. Not just a few young bucks busting loose, but organized raids that seem to be going after specific items.

"Then, too, there have been more than a

dozen killings of Indians on this reservation, and more than 50 Indians have starved to death here. Something is wrong and the Bureau of Indian Affairs won't touch it."

"Yeah, because of former vice presidential candidate Hirum Saterlee. Half of Kansas is afraid of him. As a politician he has more clout than the president himself."

"Phil is concerned because when the renegades and the organized raiders leave the reservation, then it's the Army's responsibility. He wants the problem cleared up so he doesn't have to bring in a couple of regiments and station them here to contain the hostiles who are supposed to be taken care of on the reservation.

"Saterlee is my target, Colonel Mason. I have to clean him up, talk him into quitting, or get enough evidence on him that I can get him convicted of high crimes and felonies and land his ass in a federal prison."

"Yeah, yeah. Now I understand," Colonel Mason said.

He reached in his desk drawer and brought out a bottle of whiskey and two glasses. "Good. Now I can relax. I've been stewing for two days wondering what you were going to nose into in my command. What will you need from me?"

"Quarters and rations, an orderly, and a

five man mounted squad who can ride with a sergeant in charge."

"Done!" Colonel Mason said, passing a glass with two fingers of whiskey in it to Colt. "For a minute there I thought I might be in trouble. Any idea how long this will take?"

"Like a war, when I win, it'll be over. A week, maybe two weeks, depending how tough a nut Saterlee is."

"He's been here over a year. He knows everyone, has about half the little town on his payroll as spies. I'm sure Saterlee knows about your orders by this time. He'll wonder the same as I did. I'll put out a paper to all officers about what your job here really is . . . to conduct a field survey on facilitating greater efficiency in moving army supplies from supplier to the men in the field. That'll keep everyone happy. And it will stop Saterlee from wondering about you."

"Fine, now how is the quarters situation?"

"I'll rank out a captain who I need to jolt up a bit. I'll have an orderly move out the captain and prepare it for you. In an hour, you can move in. By then I'll have a sergeant for you and you can have him select the men he wants, depending on what you'll need them to be doing. We're long on pencil pushers here and short on combat troopers. But I'm sure we can find some."

"You read my thoughts, Colonel." Colt sipped the whiskey, then tossed down the last of it. "One more small problem."

Colonel Mason looked up concerned.

Colt held up his glass. "Can we try that again, my damn glass is empty."

2

Hirum Saterlee sat in his Indian Agent's house on the Cimarron Kiowa–Comanche Reservation and drummed his fingers on the rough wooden table. He was used to better. He sighed and stared around the cabin, which was really little better than a shack.

He had been a guest in the Jefferson room in the White House in Washington, for God's sakes! How had he fallen so low that he had to take a job as an Indian Agent? Hirum knew it was the best job he could get from the government after he lost the general election as the Vice Presidential candidate. That was when he couldn't get elected as a senator from Illinois after he had given up his house seat to run on the national ticket.

Hirum sipped from a glass holding three fingers of Tennessee whiskey. He was a large man given to overeating and underexercising. He stood six feet even and weighed down a scale to the 245 pound mark. Hirum's girth was well clothed — he always prided himself on being one of the best dressed Congressmen in Washington where he had served as a Congressman for sixteen years.

He had a great brush of white hair which billowed around his head but generally was combed backward. Hirum wore a white moustache as well which made him look considerably older than he was. He liked the effect and had always figured that some day it would help propel him into the U.S. Senate and perhaps the White House. Now he'd had his shot and failed.

Hirum squinted his weak brown eyes to see the time. Ten-fifteen in the evening. His bed time. This past year his face had taken on more "character" lines than he had seen in ten years. The political campaign had started it. There had been so many glorious high experiences, such a peak surge of emotion when he had been named by the convention as the party's vice presidential candidate.

But that had been followed shortly thereafter by such agony, such terrible stories about him in the press, and such vicious attacks by the other party, that he had soon learned that such highs could be quickly balanced by terrible lows.

Damn! The fortunes of war and politics! At least his wife was in Chicago.

He watched the slender Comanche girl, Bright Night, as she rocked in her favorite place, the rocking chair next to the fire-place. She was his housekeeper, his cook, his companion. She spoke only a little English. She always said "Yes." It was the way he liked a sleek young girl.

The young Comanche was an animal in bed, he would give her that. He had taught her to perform the rituals of lovemaking exactly as he enjoyed them most.

He snorted and looked back at the fire. He had been here for a year. At least the Indians had not been too troublesome. They kept complaining that they were not getting their rations and the compensation provided for in their agreement to move to the reservation two years ago.

Too bad! This was a fat goose that needed plucking and he would go right on taking as much as he could for as long as he could. He thought of the metal strong box under the floor boards. Over the past year he had managed to "liberate" over four thousand dollars from the supplies and compensation it was his job to distribute to the savages.

Hell, what they didn't know, they couldn't complain about. The stupid savages had signed the treaty to come to the reservation, but only one or two of the chiefs knew what it said or what they were supposed to get.

Most Indians signed peace treaties when offered gifts. They signed to get the gifts and usually had no idea what the paper said. They cared even less. That was why peace treaties with these savages would never work.

Hirum grinned. He'd done right well so far. But the big strikes were coming soon. A major shipment of food, blankets and a few farming tools for the reservation was due in soon. Ten wagon loads! The wagons alone would be worth two thousand dollars! And if they pulled them with mules! Mules were worth $200 a pair and there would be six pair per wagon! Christ, he couldn't even think about that much money.

He tried. Six times $200 would be $1,200 and then that figure times ten would be . . . Great July Morning! That would be $12,000!

The idea of that much money sobered him. But these wagons would be pulled by bulls, he was sure. So something would have to be done with the mule skinners or bullwhackers who brought in the goods. He'd come to terms with that.

It was only a hundred and twenty-five miles from the railroad at Fort Hays down to the reservation. Easy trip in eight days at 15 miles a day. Hirum began to plot how he would assault the wagon train. He was determined to attack it and steal the entire shipment before it arrived at the reservation. Then he could report it as lost en route and covert the total amount of goods, wagons and teams to his own uses!

There would be no army escort. This was fairly peaceful country. No need for soldiers. Good. He would work out his plans. Short Knife would help. The savage could read and write, of all things! But he was thoroughly a Comanche again. He would be the key to the attack on the wagon train.

Hirum Saterlee pushed another log on the fire and reached over and caressed the Indian girl's full breasts. He had not always been in such a lowly position in government.

Crandal and Saterlee for United States President and Vice President! There had been banners, there had been parties and speeches, there had been six months of campaigning for the presidency and vice presidency of the United States of America! That was heady stuff for a Congressman from Chicago serving his sixth term.

The politicians at the convention had picked James P. Crandal of Massachusetts early on to be the nominee for President. Then they had struggled to find the right man to team with him to swing in the most votes. At last they picked Hirum Saterlee, a workhorse in the party, a loyal party voter in Congress, and someone from the wilds of Illinois who could swing in a lot of independent voters from that state and all over the growing, important West.

No politician these days even considered what the South wanted. The bloody confederacy states would have to take what was given them and try to win back their honor in both parties.

Hirum lit his pipe. Bright Night hurried over with more tobacco and then sat on his lap and snuggled against him. She had learned quickly what he wanted, and when. Slowly she pulled off the beaded doeskin top she wore. He had always been easily excited by a woman's bare breasts. She shook her shoulders so her breasts jiggled and Hirum chuckled, tossed her off his lap and led her into the only other room in the cabin, his bedroom.

Hirum was 48 years old. He had forgotten what fresh, vigorous and *young* sexual play could be. She always exhausted him and demanded three or four couplings. Hirum grinned. He would simply have to put up with such outlandish behavior.

As he stretched out on the bed he went

over the Presidential campaign again. Everyone thought he and Crandal were ahead — surveys, talk on the street, stories in the biggest newspapers.

Then the momentum began to shift ever so slowly. A bad bill in Congress affecting the shipping people. One of his bills that went against what some of the farmers wanted had cost them hundreds of thousands of votes.

He had counted on fifteen years of friendships forged in Congress and around the country to provide a lot of vote-getting power. He had been wrong.

Somehow it had gotten away from them.

When the final votes were counted, Crandal and Saterlee had polled only 32 percent of the vote.

Losing the election had hurt him right down to his toes. He had no job in government. His party was out of power. He went, hat in hand, to everyone he knew in Washington who might help him . . . but to no avail.

At last he changed his party alliance and got shuffled in as an Indian Agent.

By damn he would make them pay! He would get his just due, one way or the other! He was going to have a hundred thousand in the bank before he quit. It might take him five more years, but he would do it someway. Damned to hell if he wouldn't!

Charlotte Albers lay in her big bed in the best house in Prairie City and stared at the ceiling. She was getting the itch again. How long had it been . . . almost a week.

"Damn," Charlotte said out loud. She didn't have to worry about anyone hearing her swear. She was alone in the big house. Six months ago she had let the cook and maid go because she got too possessive.

Charlotte hadn't realized when she married him that Walter A. Albers was so close to being worn out. A month of lovemaking had finished him. Now he couldn't even get it hard. She wasn't sure what they called it or what caused the problem, but it had a predictable effect on her. First she had blamed herself, it was all her fault.

He convinced her that it was not.

For a week she had cried. Then she went out and went to bed with the first cowboy she met. After that she had been a little more selective.

Frances, the cook and maid, had been sympathetic. Too sympathetic. Charlotte hadn't minded playing around a little with the big, healthy German–Dutch girl. They had loved each other a few times, then

Frances demanded more and more and Charlotte had at last put a stop to it, telling the big woman that she really preferred men. She fired Frances and they both agreed that she should leave town.

Charlotte was not a raving beauty, she knew that. But she was only 23 years old, she still had a lean, sleek body. Sure her hips were a little big but she had the bust line to match them. She had brown hair around her shoulders and what she called "sensitive" brown eyes, a little nose and a cupid mouth. She had never found any problem getting a man into her bed when she really tried.

"Oh, damn!" Charlotte threw off the sheet and stood. She would go shopping, maybe find a new dress or a blouse, even a scarf. She wanted to *buy* something.

Charlotte dressed carefully, selecting a full skirt and a blouse that fit snugly around her breasts. She never objected to showing off her breasts just a little. She had a good body and she wanted the men she saw to know it.

Charlotte put a tiny blush of color on her cheeks and rubbed it in well so it didn't look like rouge, then added some red to her lips and surveyed the effect. Yes.

The big house she lived in had twelve

rooms, five upstairs and seven down. One upstairs was for the maid/cook, but now that was empty.

She went out the front door and down the concrete sidewalk to the street. A white picket fence two feet tall with pointed tops circled their front yard. Walter had seeded it in the spring and now it was lush green. The street was only dirt and there was no proper sidewalk. In time they would come. Like Chicago. She had liked Chicago.

The corner house was only a block from Main Street and that was only three blocks long. She walked to Main and stepped gratefully onto the boardwalk. She was in front of the Plains Hotel.

Charlotte smiled. Now and then she came to the Plains in the evening. There was almost always a poker game going in one of the rooms off the lobby. It was the one place where a lady could play cards and not totally besmirch her reputation. She had never entered a saloon in town and never would.

Next door she paused in front of the drug store. She had thought of getting some laudanum. Old Doc Casemore had given her a prescription for it six months ago. She had broken down and told him Walter's condition, and Doc Casemore actually had tears in his eyes as he listened.

He said it was a terrible waste, a pretty young thing like her and old Walter's equipment not working. He had given her the laudanum then for depression. He told her if she ever had a real need for . . . for male companionship, it might be best for her health if she simply went ahead and made love with someone. It was a medical decision he was giving her, he had added quickly, not a moral one.

She went into the drug store now and told Link behind the counter that she needed a refill on the last prescription. He didn't remember. She told him and he brought her a small bottle, two ounces. She shrugged, paid for it and put it in her reticule.

Link told her when she first bought it what laudanum was. He said it was a tincture of opium and she should be careful not to use to much of it or too often.

"I had a man in Jefferson who got so he needed more and more of it when he had a hand amputated. Finally he couldn't get along without it, even though his pain had gone. One night he broke in and stole all I had. I guess he took too much all at once because he killed himself with the laudanum that same night."

She promised him she would be careful. When she was so upset about Walter and so . . . so needing a man . . . it did help to ease the pressure and the pain. It put her in a nice cozy, soft and fuzzy mood and she didn't worry about much of anything for several hours.

Now she checked out the General Store. There usually were some women there sitting on a long bench near the notions and bolts of cloth. The farm and city women could gather and chat about things and just talk for company's sakes after being alone on a farm or ranch for a week or a month.

Today there were three town women talking about the benefits of the new gingham cloth that had come in. There were seven different patterns!

Charlotte said hello to them, then moved to the kitchenware section of the store but decided not to get anything new.

Outside on the boardwalk again, she saw a man walk by whom she hadn't noticed in town before. He was at least six-three, and lean with the face of an outdoorsman, sun and wind burned. He had a confident stride and carried a six-gun on his right hip. The more she watched him, the more she figured he was a soldier, probably an officer in town in his civilian clothes.

She sat in a chair in the shade near the hardware store and watched the man. He seemed to be going into several stores. She could not figure out what he was doing, or what he might be trying to buy.

A small smile brightened Charlotte's face. It was a terribly wicked idea, but she stood and walked down the boardwalk. She had been in and out of three stores before she saw him talking with the clerk at the gun counter of the general store.

Charlotte walked past him, caught a slight fragrance of soap and a touch of bay rum from an aftershave. She smiled. Not many men used fancy aftershave out here in the wilds of Kansas. It could be a good sign.

Here it was nearly noon. Would he eat in town? She guessed that he would.

The man turned and Charlotte looked at him squarely for a moment, then moved on past. He had the deepest brown eyes she had ever seen, and a moustache. At once she had liked his face. He had started to smile when she looked away and hurried past. She smiled as she walked out of the store. Whoever the man was, he would remember her.

For just a moment it gave her a thrill, a lift, and a sudden dampness under her skirt. She grinned openly now and hurried down the block to the dressmaker. She was going to order a new dress! That would really put her in a good mood!

3

Earlier that same morning, Lieutenant Colonel Colt Harding had met with the sergeant assigned him, a veteran of 12 years in the service by the name of Efrem Dunwoody.

Colt met the Sergeant in his quarters and stared at the gaunt figure for a moment. He was one of those troopers who seemed on the brink of falling over dead: ashen face, deep sunk eyes, hair brown and gray and stringy with a slouch for posture and a skinny frame that seemed filled out by an army blue shirt.

But from long experience, Colt also knew that such troopers, especially if they had survived army life for a while and if they had any rank at all, were some of the toughest and best soldiers in the world.

"Good morning, Sergeant. My name is Harding, seems like we'll be working together for a few weeks."

"Yes sir. I'm glad to be with you, sir."

"I understand you know the country around and about the fort for fifteen miles or so. That might come in handy. You've been to the reservation and to the Agency buildings?"

Sergeant Dunwoody nodded.

"Good. You've had fighting experience?"

"Yes sir. More than a little. I was at Fredericksburg with the 79th New York. Got ourselves starved out and shot full of holes. Them rebels lead rounds did hurt a mite."

"I had a small piece of that one myself, Dunwoody. What I want you to do this morning is to pick out six good men, all with combat experience, all good shots, and men who you can depend on. I'll give you an order to take to the men's Commanding Officers that will release them on Temporary Duty to me."

"Yes sir, I have some men in mind."

"Good. Get yourselves quartered together, then go to the quartermaster and get outfitted with horses and trail gear for a squad of cavalry. We may be doing some riding soon. That should keep you busy the rest of the morning."

"Yes, sir. All I'll need is your authorization. I'll check with the First Sergeant, if it's all right with you."

"Go through whatever chain of command you need to, Sergeant. Just get it done and have those men ready to ride by sundown."

"Yes sir."

Sergeant Dunwoody saluted, did a

snappy about face and floated rather than walked out the door. He was absolutely the best example of skin and bones Colt had ever seen. Take the man's uniform off and he'd fall into a mass of disconnected bones, raw sinew and bloodless flesh.

Colt called for his horse, then put on a set of civilian clothes he always carried, and rode into town. He knew little of the village of Prairie City, except that it had about 500 people and served the ranchers and farmers in this area of the Cimarron River.

Before Colt left Fort Leavenworth for this assignment, he had read some reports by the Bureau of Indian Affairs on recent cases of fraud and misappropriation of funds by Indian Agents. In almost every case there had been an arrangement with one or more of the stores in the nearby towns to buy what had been stolen from the government supplies that were allocated to the various tribes. Colt needed a good reading on the local merchants.

Colt made his first stop the Merchant's Bank of Prairie City. The banker was stuffy but proper.

"Good morning, sir. My name is Walter Albers. I'm president and cashier of this bank. How may I help you?"

"Mr. Albers, it's good to meet you. I'm in

town for a month or two doing a survey for the U.S. Army, Quartermaster Division out at Fort Larson. I like to look around each town I'm in. Banks are a favorite of mine. My father was a banker and the business has always held a fascination for me."

Walter Albers almost smiled, but not quite. "Well, welcome to Prairie City. Our small establishment here does not have the latest innovations in the business, but we try to keep up. We've just opened what we call Safe Boxes for individual customers. Are you familiar with them?"

Colt said he wasn't and the man took Colt into the walk-in vault and showed him a stack of metal boxes, each about the size of a shoe box, and each with two locks.

"We call them safe boxes because it takes two keys to open any box. One key is kept by the box renter, and a second here at the bank. When the box owner identifies himself, and we assure ourselves he is the rightful person, then we both take our keys and open the box. At that point the banker retires and the renter of the box can put things in or take them out. We think this idea is going to catch on with the general public."

"Sounds like a good idea. Oh, a question. With all the troops out at the fort, do they generate any business for you? Savings accounts, anything like that?"

"Not enough to mention. One or two of the officers have had small accounts with us from time to time, but that's about the most of it."

"Same thing must be true for the reservation and the Indian Agency then," Colt said.

Mr. Albers came close to chuckling. "Indians don't even know what money is and they don't have any so they don't need a bank. I think we do have a private account for the Agent himself. Of course, the main business is done in credits from the Bureau of Indian Affairs."

"Yes, of course. I have to start thinking Western a little more, I'm afraid. Well, it was good talking with you. I better not take up any more of your time."

Albers gave Colt a limp handshake as he left.

Colt's judgment came quickly. Albers was stodgy, four square honest, solid, a model citizen, and he would have absolutely nothing to do with shady dealings by the Indian Agent.

Two doors down, Colt stopped in at the J. A. Overbay General Store. He wandered around amazed at the variety of goods that could be brought in by freight wagon. He looked at the display of guns and to make his visit more realistic, he asked to buy a box of .45 rounds.

As the clerk got them for him, an attractive woman walked toward Colt. She stared directly at him. Her deep brown eyes seemed to challenge him for a second, then she walked past. She was slender, taller than most women, and had an interesting walk that left Colt starting after her.

Colt recovered as the clerk brought the rounds. He checked the head stamp on them, approved the make and date, and paid the bill.

"Are you the owner here?" Colt asked as he handed over the cash.

"Man and boy for almost eight years now," J. A. Overbay said. "Fact is, I put up the second store in this young town. Some big Eastern hotshot came out and plotted out the whole town, then tried to sell it. He was right, this area needed a town, but he figured there should be 5,000 people here, when 500 is more than enough."

"Things look prosperous," Colt said.

"Long as the price of beef stays up," Overbay said.

Colt saw a counter that had a glass top and a display of several pieces of jewelry in it. He was sure that they were not new.

Some of the gold settings were tarnished.

"Jewelry. Don't often see goods that valuable in a general store."

"True," Overbay said. "Fact is, I'm a sucker for a hard luck story. This little widow lady needed to go back East to be with her family. Going back to die, she said. So I bought the jewelry and now I'm stuck with it."

"That can happen," Colt said.

Then he saw more goods that were not new: tools mostly, good carpenter tools and a pair of bridles. When Overbay handed Colt back his change he did not count it out. Colt looked down and pushed the change around.

"Oh, damn, I owe you another quarter," Overbay said, looking down at the change. He pulled one out of a change drawer and Colt pocketed the coins.

"Thanks," Colt said. "I might wander around a little and see if there's anything else I need."

Colt did, found more used equipment and merchandise that could have come from a farm sale, or it could have been stolen in an Indian raid. There were more than ten ways to make cash money from an Indian Agency job and he was getting the idea that Agent Saterlee knew them all.

Colt checked on several more stores and shops, found no more used merchandise. Then he went to the small building between the barbershop and the millinery store. It was the Prairie City Town Office. Inside was the Town Marshal and his two-cell lock up.

It would be easiest to operate a large scale fraud if Saterlee owned the local law man. In this case a Town Marshal, since this was not a county seat where they would have an elected sheriff.

Colt stepped through the door and saw a man about sixty nod and put down the local newspaper.

"Morning, stranger. What can I do for you?"

"Are you the Town Marshal?"

"Yep."

"Good, we need to have a talk."

The marshal waved him in and Colt sat down in a chair beside a scarred desk. The Marshal was not wearing a gun. Bad sign, Colt decided.

"My name is Colt Harding."

"Yep, and I'm Marshal Tom Powell. What can I help you with?"

Not much, Colt thought, but he didn't say it. "I've just arrived out at the fort to look into a few matters that might have some connection to the town. I was wondering if you've seen anything unusual happening around town lately?"

"Not a thing. This is a quiet place, not one of your cattle drive towns. Just a few farmers, a few ranchers, and no bad blood in a bucketful."

"Glad to hear that. The reservation cause you any problems?"

"Once in a green moon some brave gets a snoot full of whiskey and starts whopping it up, but nothing serious. We ain't had a hanging offense in town for . . . well . . . about three years, I guess. Then it was some Eastern gent who shot his wife. We hung him."

"Soldiers don't bother you any?"

"Soldiers don't have no cash money to spend so they don't come to town. What can they do? Can't even get drunk. Most of them stay around the fort."

Colt stood. "Fine, Marshal. That's what I wanted to know. The quieter a town near an Army fort is, the better we like it. Oh, I'd appreciate it if you didn't mention anything about what we've said."

"Don't intend to."

"Thanks for the chat."

"Think nothing of it," Marshal Powell said.

As Colt closed the door behind him, he saw the lawman push his hat down over his eyes, lift his feet to the edge of the desk and settle into the chair. Colt knew he would get very little help from the marshal, even if he needed it. He was just marking time. The town council probably told him to keep things quiet, the quieter the better.

Colt was hungry. He had missed morning chow at the officers' mess. He looked at the Waterbury pocket watch he carried. Ten minutes after noon. He headed for the Plains Hotel because he knew it had a dining room. Usually the hotel in a small town had the best food. He hoped that was true here.

Ten minutes later, Colt had ordered his meal and sat at a table for two waiting for his food. He had been looking out the window but someone walked by his chair and he glanced up. It was the same woman he had seen in the general store. She paused beside one table, then turned and came back toward where he sat.

She looked directly at him and a small smile curved around her mouth as she stopped beside his table.

"Sir, it's so crowded in here today, I wonder if I could impose on you to share your table with me."

Colt grinned as he stood. It was one of the oldest lines in the book. He nodded gravely.

"Rush hour at the tables is terrible. Please sit down. It's my pleasure, really."

Colt's first impression had been right. She was the same woman who had looked so frankly at him in the store. Her liquid brown eyes were framed by soft brown hair close around her face.

"I've ordered, what would you like?"

"Just some coffee. I'm a light eater."

"Do you come here often, or just when it's crowded?"

She laughed softly and looked away. "Wasn't that terrible of me? I get these urges sometimes to say hello to someone, and usually I just do it. How else do you meet nice people?"

"I'm glad you did. I'm new in town and you can help me. What is the best restaurant? I saw one called Molly's."

"She has the best food, and this is next. Neither one is anything like the famous eating places in Chicago."

"You're from Chicago?"

"No, but I visited there."

She paused and stared at him with an open, fragile frankness. "My name is Charlotte," she said.

"I'm Colt."

"You staying here at the hotel?"

"Why?"

"I thought maybe we could go to your room and look at the wallpaper. . . or something." She smiled and he could see the tension, the need, the longing, mirrored there. "Do I have to draw a picture for you?"

"No. But I don't have a room."

The waitress brought his dinner, a big soup plate filled with beef stew and large slabs of bread. When the waitress left, Charlotte smiled again.

"You could always go rent one, and tell me the number. . . ."

"Charlotte, I'm a married man."

"So what? I'm married, too."

"I'm sorry, Charlotte. You picked the wrong man."

He hesitated. "You're still welcome to stay for coffee, or for dinner."

The need, the longing, the wanting, broke through her faint smile. Her face worked for a moment, then she sighed and stood. "No, Colt. I really can't do that. You're probably a very good person, but at this moment I hate you."

Her voice was now edged with steel and had a rancor at the end that surprised Colt. Charlotte stepped away from the table, turned and walked away without looking back.

The beef stew had lost its appeal. Colt knew the lady had some problems, but he couldn't solve the hurts of the whole world. He buttered a slice of the whole wheat bread and salted it lightly, then ate. Gradually, he forgot the hurting woman and settled down to the best beef stew he had tasted in months.

Colt spent the rest of the afternoon walking the town. He found little unusual. He spent some time at the *Advocate*, the small newspaper that came out twice a month "or whenever the news warranted it." What that meant, Colt was sure, was whenever there was enough advertising to pay the costs of producing and delivering the paper.

That evening he stayed in his quarters going over another report of fraud in an Indian Agency compiled by the Bureau of Indian Affairs. There were definite patterns of what usually was stolen and how it was disposed of.

While Colt had been eating his noon time beef stew, Slade Rogers unpacked goods in the Prairie City Hardware store just down the block. Slade did not have his headache now. When he got the headache, the agonizing pain that felt like a hot poker through his brain, he was not entirely sure what he did.

There were only fragments and flashes of memory of those times. He knew something terrible happened. Many times he had come back to reality in a strange place — beside a trail, maybe a mile from town, or on the horse that he owned and kept at the livery.

Slade knew he drank. He went to one of the saloons almost every night because he had no family to go home to. In fact, he had no home, just a room that Mr. Rasmussen had built for him in the hardware store's back room. He was thirty-six years old with no family, no home, and a bleak future.

Usually, he drank more when he got the head pain. He wasn't sure now if the drinking caused the pain, or if he drank more because of the agony it created. They were tied together somehow.

He opened a heavy cardboard box and took out small brown boxes that had green labels. Stove Bolts 1/8" by 2", Stove Bolts 3/16" by 3".

Slade had learned as much about the hardware business as he could. That meant he could use much of his farmer's understanding of simple farm tools and his carpenter background to lay in a store of knowledge about all tools and fasteners and the rest of the thousands of items in a complete hardware.

A touch of pain throbbed through his head. Slade ripped open another box. He would not think about his dead wife. He would not think about his mutilated children or his burned-to-the-ground house and barn. He would not!

The agony of the terrible pain staggered him for a moment. He slapped his head with both hands three times, then with tears in his eyes he took a deep breath and felt the pain easing. Five minutes later it was gone.

Slade took the boxes of stove bolts out to the front of the store and put them on the shelf where the rest of the green label boxes were. He filled them into the slots by size and usually found a slot where they were out of that size. He loved the hardware store work.

Karl Rasmussen had seen Slade hitting himself. He knew the signs. He found Slade at the bolt shelves and held out the small bottle.

"Doc said if the pain gets too bad you should take some of this. It's medicine. Old Doc Casemore wouldn't give you anything that would hurt you. Now take the bottle."

Slade shook his head. "I know what that is, Karl. I told you ten times before. It's the devil's own juice and I won't take any of it. It comes from the opium poppy. That's what the Chinese smoke in their dens. I wouldn't be any good to anybody if I started to take that laudanum stuff. You just keep it, Karl."

"Slade, I still worry about you. Once I came to talk to you about something and I couldn't find you anywhere in town. None of the saloons, or your room. Still don't know where you were."

"I came back to work the next day, didn't I?"

"Yes, but when I asked you where you had been all night, you told me you didn't know."

"I'm fine, Karl. You don't have to worry about me. I'm getting better all the time. You should order some new carriage bolts. We're short on some of the half-inchers. Lots of farmers use them in their new plows and harrows."

Karl looked at the shelf. "You're right, Slade. I'll get my want book right now and put it down."

Slade grinned. Yeah, he was getting better all the time.

Just after midnight a man walked two heavily loaded pack mules down a trail that led from the reservation. He wore white man's clothes, had a pistol on a gun belt, and prodded the two pack mules along the trail at a fast pace.

A half hour later he had traveled the two miles to Prairie City and come into town through the least built up area. He took the side streets until he could turn down the alley behind Main Street. At the door of the J. A. Overbay General Store he brought the mules to a stop.

A shadow came away from deeper shadows, gave a sign, and then opened the door of the general store. Quickly the mules were unloaded. On one were two hundred pounds of dry beans. On the other were six axes, two five foot crosscut saws, and two hundred pounds of white flour.

The man at the back door of the store reached in his pocket and took out several bills. He counted them out to the man who had brought the goods. Then without another spoken word, he turned and went back inside the store and threw the bolt across the door.

Short Knife looked from under his white man's hat and glowered. The merchant had thousands of dollars inside, he was sure. One of these days, on a delivery just like this, he would force the man inside, rob him of every cent he had, kill the white trash and ride his war pony deep into the wilderness and find the Comanches who had not come to the blanket.

Some day!

Short Knife pushed the bills into his pocket and rode one of the mules as he hurried back to the reservation.

He would get paid part of the money for his delivery mission. Lately he had asked for half, but Saterlee had given him only one quarter of it. Saterlee wasn't sure if Short Knife knew the difference between half and a quarter, and Short Knife wasn't going to tell him.

The same night when he would rob the store owner, he would also rob the Indian Agent of all of his illegal gains. Short Knife knew about the small safe the Agent used and the metal box under the floor.

One of these days!

4

Frank Ingram walked beside the lead bulls in the eight-team string of animals pulling the heavy freight wagon. It was the old-type wagon, a single unit loaded down with more than two tons of food and equipment.

Frank was 23, had grown up on a farm in Iowa and took to bullwhacking naturally. It was one way to see more of the world than the hindside of a plow mule. He didn't mind walking. His long, black bull-snake sang out as he cracked it over the head of the offside lead steer turning the animal to the left so the wagon would angle down the slight draw and avoid the ridgeline of a small rise a mile or so ahead.

The wagonmaster rode past on his pinto pony, judged the direction and nodded. His name was Rash. That's the only name he gave and the only one they knew. He was a tough one, looked like he enjoyed eating nails for breakfast and spitting them out at you like a repeating Spencer rifle if he was unhappy. Which he was most of the time, Frank decided.

Frank grinned. He was feeling good today

in spite of the rain squall last night that had soaked everything. He'd huddled under the wagon and tucked his poncho around himself but still got soaked in twenty minutes. Today was bright and clear.

He'd signed on at Fort Hays and helped them unload the rail car and stuff the ten big Studebaker wagons. It was only a trip of 125 miles, eight, maybe nine days. Then he'd probably drive back empty. Not much to haul in from this far south side of Kansas next to the Nations.

Frank watched the country ahead. Nothing but the gently rolling Kansas prairie. A few trees here and there fringing a small creek or river. He had no idea why anyone would want to live in such a god-forsaken place as southern Kansas. Now Iowa, there was a place with respectable farms and little towns. When he got back from this trip he had about decided to head back to Iowa.

If Wilma Hotchkiss wasn't married yet, he was gonna propose and get married and find a little farm he could buy and settle himself down. It was about time. He was going on twenty-three years old.

Rash Johnson sat his horse just behind the lead wagon and surveyed his ten-rig train. Not much of a trip, not much of a train, but a man had to keep busy. He'd taken this job because there wasn't a better one.

The days of the long freight wagon trains were about gone. Damn railroad had done that deed! Now the main work was moving goods from a railroad line into towns and camps off the beaten routes. Rash sighed and checked the surrounding skyline. He saw nothing to put him on edge, but he'd been skitterish all morning without knowing why.

It felt as if somebody was watching him. Never had that feeling so strong before. As if somebody was watching and waiting. They couldn't be more than a dozen miles outside of a little town called Prairie City which was a mile or so from the Indian Agency they were headed for.

Rash took off his hat and rubbed midday sweat off his headband. Not exactly a scorcher, but warm enough. So far, so good. He'd lost only two bulls up to now so most of the spares they drove along at the end of the train had not been needed. That was fine with him. If he lost no more than two he'd get a ten dollar bonus.

The lead wagon dipped into the shallow draw that would lead eventually to a branch of the Cimarron River. Ten minutes later all the wagons were in the draw heading for the flatter lands ahead.

A rifle shot blasted into the Kansas plains stillness.

Rash heard it at once, and a troubled cry from the lead bullwhacker. Rash spurred his pinto forward from the second wagon and soon saw the problem. The lead bull on the first wagon was down in its traces and not moving.

He stood in his stirrups and stared around at the slight rise on both sides of the draw but saw nothing. Rash spurred on to the front of the six teams of steers and waved at the bullwhacker to get down.

Another rifle shot cracked and at the same time, Rash felt the slug slam into his horse. It had been meant for him but missed and caught the pinto in the side of the head. The horse went down and Rash jumped off the fatally wounded animal. He ran between the nearest steers in harness.

"Frank! In here!" Rash bellowed. Frank ran a dozen feet and slid in beside his trail boss.

"What the hell?" Frank asked.

"Trouble," Rash said. "I still don't see nobody."

Just as he said it, eleven horses came over the rise and rode hard at the strung out supply train and the drivers.

"Indians!" Rash said.

At first the eleven Comanches circled the long train, taking shots at the drivers who had hidden behind wagon wheels or between their animals. One bullwhacker, a kid of only eighteen, took a slug in the chest on the first ride-by of the Comanches. He died almost instantly.

"Stay down!" Rash bellowed to the next bullwhacker. "Pass the word. Keep your head down. Maybe they'll leave."

Rash leveled in with his Remington six-gun and fired but missed the Indian.

"What the hell they want?" Frank asked as he fired a round from his iron.

"The goods, the food, I'd guess," Rash said. He fired again and an Indian pony screamed as the bullet hit it in the hind quarters.

Frank looked at him in surprise.

"Hell, I never said I was good with a gun," Rash snapped. "Let's figure out how we can stay alive."

The bullwhackers had stashed their blanket rolls and personal gear on the front of their wagons. That's also where they carried their spare ammunition. There were plenty of chances to get the rounds. Frank had a rifle with him and he gave it to Rash.

Again and again the Indians rode around the train. They used rifles, but shooting a rifle from a moving horse was a skill the Comanches had not learned well. After a half hour of riding and shooting, the Comanches pulled back. Rash ran from one wagon to the next and soon found out that he had one bullwhacker dead and another wounded in the shoulder.

Rash was no general, but he pulled all nine of his men together. There was no time to circle the wagons. He positioned the nine men among the steers pulling the number four wagon.

"We'll fire at the same Indian if they do the circling again," Rash said. "That way we should be able to knock down some of the bastards and convince them to leave."

The Comanches had changed their plans, too. They dropped off their horses now and ran to the abandoned first wagon, then four of them ran to the second wagon and began firing at the men around the fourth.

As they fired, four more Indians ran to the third wagon and now had the men in pistol range.

Two Comanches lifted up from the third wagon and raced for the cover provided by the lead bulls on the fourth wagon.

"Now!" Rash roared and ten guns fired, all pistols but one. One of the Indians was spun around by a bullet, then was hit again as a pistol round tore through his left eye and out the top of his head.

The other Indian reached the lead team. Frank put a sixth round in his weapon as he reloaded it, then began working slowly through the harnessed animals toward the Indian at the lead team.

Frank had moved only past two steers when a pistol shot roared. The slug caught Frank in the shoulder and threw him back three feet. He screeched in pain, then fired twice at the Comanche and saw one of his rounds hit the red man's arm. But too late he knew he was still a target.

A pistol round blasted from the Indian's gun-that-fires-six-times and blew away half of Frank's face and the rest of his life.

Rash stood and with the rifle shot the second Indian who had penetrated the teams of oxen on the fourth wagon. The round hit him in the chest and he flopped over backwards and never moved.

Three mounted Indians galloped in from the right, screaming and shooting their rifles. They stayed back out of pistol range and sent a deadly fire into the insecure haven the bullwhackers had found.

"Back to the wagon!" Rash screamed and the men worked their way back to the firmer protection of the sides of the wagon and the wagon wheels. Rash used his knife to slash the top loose on the wagon and pulled down wooden boxes of goods they could use to build a small fort under the wagon.

The rifles continued to crack from outside, and another bullwhacker screamed and fell into the dirt dead of a head shot.

A half hour later Rash had built a solid fort under the fourth wagon. He had used the rifle effectively, driving the Indian riflemen back to cover twice. Now they sneaked up again and he blasted, hitting one of the braves in the leg. That brought a volley of ten shots from the Indian rifles. But the slugs pounded into the wooden crates and never penetrated the second board inside.

Now there were riflemen on both sides of them.

"They ain't shooting the steers," one of the whackers said. "Must mean they want to drive them away. Want the damn goods, not us. Why don't we just scoot off and let them have the lot!"

" 'Cause, Millhouse, then we don't get our pay," Rash shouted. "You signed the paper. We lose the shipment, we don't get paid."

"Dead men can't spend wages," the whacker called Millhouse said.

"Suit yourself," Rash said. "I ain't no

damn general, but looks to me like we stand a better chance right here."

"Maybe, maybe not," Millhouse challenged. "Me, I aim to try it in the other direction. Anybody want to leave with me?"

He looked around. Three of the bullwhackers were dead. That left seven and the boss made it eight.

One of the men shrugged. "I'll stay here," he said.

Most nodded. One kid about eighteen frowned, then at last nodded. "I'll go. We slip through the teams they might not see us until we're out and past the tenth wagon."

"Might," Rash said. "You could wait until dark."

"Be dead by dark," Millhouse said. "Come on, Willy, let's go. Put a sixth round in your iron and let's leave these dead men."

Rash watched them as they got ready to move. "We can at least give them some cover fire," he said.

The six men left under the wagon each fired four rounds toward the Indian rifles. They weren't sure if it did any good. Rash saw Millhouse scamper from the back of the wagon to the fifth set of bulls pulling the wagon behind.

Then Willy tried it. By then the Indians had spotted the try and were ready. Six rifles rounds searched for his skin. Two found it just before he got the lead bulls. Willy plowed into the dirt and sand of the Kansas plains and never moved.

Millhouse watched the man for a minute, then shrugged and worked his way between the pairs of steers, keeping his head low. He tried to watch for the savages. So far he hadn't seen any. He paused at the last team, then surged under the wagon and crawled from one wheel to the next.

Good, no shots were coming his way. He crawled to the back of the wagon and crouched, ready to sprint to the next team of oxen about twenty yards behind. Just as he rose up and took his first running step, a Comanche screamed and jumped on his back from the top of the loaded wagon.

Millhouse and the Indian warrior tumbled to the ground and rolled. When they stopped, the Comanche had his knife pressed against Millhouse's throat. Silently, Millhouse held up his revolver by the barrel offering it to the savage.

"You think I'm only a stupid Indian?" Short Knife bellowed at Millhouse in perfect English.

Millhouse jolted in surprise. "Christ! You talk English. Let me up, I'll pay you plenty. Just let me run out in the prairie."

Short Knife shrugged. "What can you pay me?"

Millhouse pointed at the weapon. "Damn good Colt, and I got a hundred rounds, and in my pocket I got four dollars I been saving for a whore in Prairie City."

Short Knife eased the knife away from Millhouse's throat and held out his hand. The bullwhacker put his revolver in the red man's hand, then dug in his jeans for the four folded dollar bills in his small leather purse. He gave the whole purse to the Indian who had moved back and now sat on the ground.

When Short Knife saw the bills, he nodded. "Go ahead," Short Knife said. "Go around this side of the teams, then the rest of my people won't see you."

Millhouse's face broke into a grin. "Thanks! Damn, thanks. I knew I could make a deal!" He looked at the next oxen. "Thanks, I better go."

Short Knife nodded. Millhouse rose up and ran doubled over toward the next team.

Short Knife lifted his rifle and shot Millhouse in the back. The first round shattered his spine and Millhouse went down dead in the Kansas dirt before he could really know what life was supposed to be all about.

Short Knife laughed. "Never trust a Comanche, white man. You learned your lesson too late."

On the edge of the small rise overlooking the stalled supply train, Indian Agent Hirum Saterlee walked up and down in a short path watching the fighting, checking his watch, then staring back at the Indians below and the wagon train. He looked up at the sun, then at his watch and shook his head.

Short Knife had circled around and now sat down in the grass beside the Agent.

Saterlee was surprised to see the Indian appear suddenly beside him. He scowled. "You said it would take only an hour. Now we can't get back to the reservation before dark."

"No hurry," Short Knife said. "They must be army fighters. We will wait until darkness and slip up on them."

"Damn, that won't be for three or four hours yet."

"Go to the stream and cool off," Short Knife said. "Sit in the water and then sit on the grass. Lots of cool."

Saterlee stared at Short Knife seriously for a moment, then he burst out laughing. "I never get used to the idea that a Comanche can have a sense of humor, Short Knife.

You are one card. Get down there and take care of the rest of those damn bullwhackers. The way we decided."

Short Knife went back to his men. Two had been killed. He had not counted on such a furious fight from the bull drivers. Now that they had killed two Comanche they all must die. That was good. Then there would be no one to say Comanche had taken the goods.

He lay near a little rise of ground with three of his men with rifles who now and then shot into the heavy boxes and just over them.

"We will wait for darkness," he told them. "No more of us need die here today."

Back in the fort under wagon number four, Rash looked at his remaining troops. They had seen the last two men killed. They had heard the scream and the talk by Millhouse. Then saw him shot down as he ran.

"Six of us left," Rash told the men. He shook his head. "This wasn't supposed to happen. A simple little drive like this. I don't know what went wrong. The Indians in this whole area are supposed to be in reservations."

A man about thirty-five who had come to make enough money to move on west looked up. He had a round in his shoulder. "Rash, we gonna get out of this alive?"

"I don't know, Nate. I just don't know. They want the wagons and the goods or they'd be burning them by now. Never could figure out the Comanche. Soon as it gets dark we'll all move out together. That way we can concentrate our fire. Their rifles won't be any good at night."

Rash nodded. "Damn right! It gets dark we'll be out of here and let the fucking savages take the wagons. Dead men can't spend their pay. Hell yes, Nate. I think we have a better than fifty/fifty chance to get out of here and live to fight another day."

Nate grinned. "Not interested in fighting, no more. Think I'll head back to St. Louis or maybe New Orleans. Tired of fighting."

"Good luck, Nate. But I'm afraid that our whole damn life is going to be one long fight."

Both sides waited for darkness. It came slowly and then at last dusk turned into blackness. The moon was waning and low in the sky. Rash and the five men moved out through a hole in the fort they had built. They walked quietly and on the side away from where the most Indians had been. With any luck. . . .

They made it twenty yards from the

wagon before Rash saw a shape in front of him. He lifted his six-gun to fire, but a searing, slashing pain grew on his neck and throat. Then he saw a flash of a red grinning face and he felt the blood cascade down from his slit-open throat. Blood pumped out his carotid arteries and his jugular vein drained used life fluid down his shirt.

"Oh, God! I'm dying!" Rash thought, then he knew he was falling. In those few parts of a second before he died, he felt a great rush of anger and pain and the white hot fire burned through his skull, blanking out all memory, all thought, all motion, all life, and he died in the Kansas soil well before his appointed time.

"Watch out!" Nate roared as he saw the shape ahead of him.

He got off three shots before a bullet blasted through his belly, shattering, ripping, tearing his intestines into a mass of bloody shreds and dumping him backward onto the ground. He hurt like he never had before.

He saw the savages then, bursting on the other four men, knives flashing, pistols blasting. One Indian went down in the filtered moonlight. A bullwhacker took a round in the chest but fought on, killing the savage who shot him only to have his head half cut off as a heavy knife from behind sliced across his throat.

Nate watched it all. It was over in only a few seconds, but it seemed like an hour. Nate held his belly closed with both hands, trying to splice back together all the vitals that had been chopped up. He knew he couldn't.

The pain hadn't really started yet. It would take him an hour to die, a terrible pain-filled hour. He wanted it over fast. They might leave him there.

He still had his hand gun. He raised it as an Indian formed in the darkness ahead of him and stepped forward. The round hit the savage in the chest. Nate fired his last three shots at flashes of other weapons in the night.

Two rounds hit Nate. Another one in the belly, then one in his chest and he slammed backwards into the grass and dirt. His arms had flung wide and he found he couldn't move them. He sighed and tasted blood in his mouth. Nate tried to cough but couldn't. The blood filled his mouth and his nose and he tried to gasp for air but only blood went down his air pipes. He choked and gasped again, then his heart stopped beating and his head rolled to one side.

Nate never saw Short Knife who lifted his

blade and sliced the white man's throat just to make sure.

The fight was over, the prize had been taken. Short Knife went through the pockets of all the white men, found only a few dollars and kept it, then ran back to the wagons. He had lost two more men and one wounded. Four of his ten killed! He should slash all the white men, but that would indicate an Indian attack. That must not be obvious.

Back at the wagons, he had men cutting out the two dead oxen and rigging the harness so the rest of the animals could pull. They wouldn't want to be driven tonight, but they would. He found the bullwhips and worked with one until he could crack it with authority. He got the lead wagon moving, then the others followed.

In an hour the ten wagons rolled forward. The four dead Comanche were tied over their horses trailing the wagons. With any luck they would be well into the reservation before it got light.

Hirum Saterlee had made them search the battle scene carefully. Every item that could point to an Indian attack had been found and picked up or destroyed. All the Indians had used firearms, so there were no tell-tale arrows or lances.

The site was clean for the inspection by someone. The bullwhackers were left where they had fallen.

Hirum smiled. He wasn't sure of the value of the shipment that had come from the Bureau of Indian Affairs, but it was substantial. Ten, maybe twenty thousand dollars worth! His entire year's pay was eleven hundred dollars. He would sell what he could, trade some, and be well on his way to becoming a rich man!

Saterlee grinned as he rode away toward the reservation. He would stay with the wagons. It was too valuable a cargo to allow Short Knife to steal it away from him. From long experience he had learned never to trust a Comanche.

Hell, Saterlee thought with a snort. He never trusted anybody!

5

Hirum Saterlee did not like riding a horse, but in this case he made an exception. He should clear eight to ten thousand dollars on these goods, as long as he could keep them hidden from the thieving Comanches.

He had worried about hiding the wagons on the reservation, but then he decided he could deal with the Comanches and the Kiowas a lot easier than some sheriff's posse or maybe an army unit. Short Knife had hunted for a small valley where none of the savages were camped. He found one about two miles from the Agency house.

As he rode along beside one of the wagons, Saterlee felt like a kid just before Christmas. All of those packages to be un-wrapped and unboxed! He was anxious to see what his day's work had produced.

For a fleeting moment he thought about the eleven white men who had gone into the Kansas dust. They had been in the wrong place when there was danger. Not Hirum Saterlee's fault, not a damn bit his fault. The savages killed those men, not Indian Agent Hirum Saterlee!

Even the bad logic quieted the nagging of his conscience. It was going to be a long ride to the reservation, then on to the small valley where Short Knife would post guards.

He knew Short Knife would steal as much as he could for himself. The vicious, murdering savage deserved it, Saterlee decided. If he had hired white men to do the job, they would have talked sooner or later no matter how well he paid them.

Yes, this was the best way. A little more food and a twenty dollar gold piece would keep Short Knife satisfied. The young Comanche was the only Indian Saterlee knew who wanted gold and paper money. Short Knife knew the value, knew what he could do with money in the future. That fact alone made Short Knife a murderously dangerous Comanche to have around.

Saterlee touched the derringer in his jacket pocket. It was a two-shot .45 caliber and loaded with solid slugs. He could stop any human ever born with two shots from that little beauty, especially if the man was within arm's reach.

Five hours later the mule train creaked and groaned across the borders of the reservation. Saterlee eased his tension just a little.

Then he could stand it no longer. He borrowed Short Knife's sharp blade and cut the tied-down canvas off one of the wagons and had it stop while he climbed on board. Then he began cutting open boxes and checking sacks of goods.

In one large cardboard box he found small white sacks filled with dried fruit. There were six or seven different kinds. He picked out a sack of dried apricots and passed them around to the Comanches who drove the train and cracked the long bullwhips.

Short Knife grinned. "Apricots!" he said. "We used to have these in Texas. Good, but I like the fresh ones better. Why don't you get us some fruit trees so we can start an orchard?"

Saterlee looked down from the wagon at the savage who now seemed like a blanket Indian.

"Didn't think you'd be on the reservation long enough to see a fruit tree grow up to produce, Short Knife."

The Comanche grinned. "Might, might not. Get us some peach trees and some apricots and apples. Somebody will be here."

He turned and rode off and Saterlee, a former member of the United States Congress and a candidate for the high office of Vice President of the United States, felt that he had just been given an order — by a savage, murdering Comanche!

He stared after Short Knife. When the project here was over, when he had milked this Agency job for all it was worth, he swore to himself that he would kill that damn Short Knife. The Indian knew too many white man's ways to be safe in a tribe. He would have to be cut down with a pair of .45 rounds!

The last mile into the small valley Saterlee rode on his horse again. He memorized the route they took, and even in the dark watched for landmarks he could use to get back here. They drove the wagons into a line, side by side. Then Saterlee showed the Indians how to unhitch the oxen.

Each man was given one of the steers to take back to his camp. One steer would supply thirty Indians with food for two days if they did it right. Some of it might be cut into strips and left in the sun to dry as jerky. He hoped these blanket Indians remembered what to do when they had too much fresh meat.

Saterlee made sure the harness was separated and saved. He also kept the rest of the steers in the upper part of the valley. There was plenty of graze there and enough water. Eventually the Comanches and Kiowas

would find them and kill them. But for a
while the Indians would all have plenty of
food.

He would use part of what he had taken
for the tribe. There was no sense in them
starving to death and charging off the reservation. Then his soft job would be over.

He checked some of the goods by torch-
light, pried the lids off some of the wooden
boxes and found axes and saws, but mostly
food. Saterlee made sure the goods remained covered on the wagons and then
told Short Knife he was going back to the
Agency house. The Indian sat on his horse
watching him.

"You said I'd earn a double eagle as well
as food," Short Knife said.

Saterlee dug into his pocket, brought out
a thin purse and took one twenty-dollar
gold piece from it.

"My last dollar, Short Knife. You drive a
hard bargain. Now I want you to stay here
and keep everyone away from the goods. I'll
be out late tomorrow afternoon and sort
through some of the merchandise. I'll bring
that Agency wagon and we can take some of
the food and deliver it to the tribes to keep
the animals contented."

"I don't mind being called an animal,
Saterlee, as long as you pay me well. You

promised me a quarter of everything on the wagons. I want my part in gold."

"I'm tired, Short Knife. Tired and cranky and I can't think straight. I need some sleep. It's almost dawn. We'll talk tomorrow. You're on guard duty, as of now. Use as many men as you want."

He rode off aways, then came back.

"Figure out a good reason those four men were killed. I don't want a big ritual burial. Try to do it quietly."

Short Knife laughed. "Comanche women wail and scream and slash their breasts at funerals. There has never been a quiet one. Now we'll have four and there'll be lots of screaming and wailing."

Saterlee nodded and rode away feeling that again the savage had won the talking confrontation and lectured the white man. The damn uppity savage would not be able to get away with that for long. Saterlee fingered the derringer in his pocket, hesitated, then rode on toward his house and his bed.

Charlotte Albers sat in her kitchen looking into the big back yard that had a picket fence all the way around it. The yard had been carefully planted with grass and now boasted bright flowers around the edges.

From time to time they had a handyman in to work on the garden and the yard. Today she watched out the window as a young man of sixteen worked on the lawn, carefully clipping around the edge of the grass. She had been surprised when he said he was sixteen when he came to work that afternoon. She had guessed he was at least eighteen. He stood taller than her own five feet six inches by half a dozen inches.

Now she watched him bend to his work. He had stripped off his shirt and she saw the muscles flex along his back. His chest was not filled out yet and his stomach was flat and hard.

"Oh, lord!" she breathed. One hand had touched her breast and she realized it was warm, starting to throb. She stood at once and went to the kitchen screen door.

"Rob! Rob, would you come here a moment."

He looked up, pushed brown hair out of his eyes and nodded. He stood and walked to the small porch.

"Come in, you're working too hard. It's time for a recess. Could I get you some cold milk and a cookie or two?"

"Oh, yes, ma'am, that would taste good. It surely is warm out there today."

She led him to the kitchen table where he

sat down and she poured a glass of milk for him from a jug she kept in the ice box. It would keep milk sweet for several days if the man brought the ice on time.

She sat across from him, nibbling on an oatmeal and raisin cookie that she had made the day before.

"Is that good?" she asked.

"Oh, yes it is, Mrs. Albers. I surely do appreciate it."

"Good. You're working so hard."

She slid her little jacket off. It was meant to come off the summer dress and left her shoulders bare except for the wide straps that held the bodice just over her breasts but showed a lot of bare skin.

He watched her a moment, grinned and went back to the milk.

"Rob, are you sweet on some girl?"

"No, ma'am."

"Come on now, Rob. A big, handsome, young man like you must have girls following him around town."

"No, ma'am." He smiled. "Course, there is this one pretty girl I surely do wish would at least say hello to me."

"Who is she, I'll have a talk with her."

"Oh, I couldn't tell you."

She brushed her skin over the top of her dress and he watched. Then she let her hand drift softly down over her breast and he never took his gaze off her hand.

"You do like girls, then, Rob."

He looked up, knowing she had caught him looking at her full breasts pushing against the fabric of her dress.

"Uh . . . oh, yes. I'm normal, I guess."

"Rob, you're far above normal, I can assure you."

He finished the milk and the cookie.

"Rob, there's something I want you to do inside for a few minutes. Down this way."

He followed her into the living room, then along a short hall to the master bedroom.

"Rob, could you move the bed over about a foot toward the wall. It's just so big and heavy for me to push."

Rob nodded. "I can do that easily." He moved the foot, then the headboard, and made sure the mattress didn't fall off the boards.

"That about right?" he asked, looking back at her.

Charlotte stood near him. She had unbuttoned the front of her dress and he saw plainly that she had nothing on under it. Her soft white skin showed between the unbuttoned front of the dress and nearly half of each of her flaring breasts.

Rob sucked in a breath and stood.

"Oh!" he said. "I . . . I guess . . . I should. . . ."

Charlotte turned and closed the bedroom door and threw a small bolt. She walked up to Rob and took his face in her hands and kissed his lips.

When she let his lips go she held his face close. "Do you like that, Rob?"

"Y . . . yes."

"Want me to do it again?"

"Uh huh."

She kissed him again, then pulled him close until her body pressed tightly against his all the way to their hips. Her breasts crushed against his chest as the dress front opened more. Her hips pushed hard against his until she felt the growing bulge at his crotch.

The kiss was hot and long and when at last she eased away from him he was nearly panting.

"I have something I'd like to show you, Rob."

"Oh . . . God!"

Charlotte pushed back the top of her dress, pulled it off her arms and let it fall around her waist. Her large breasts swung out and Rob stared at them. He had never seen a woman's breasts before, never.

"I know exactly what you want, Rob. I

know what you want to do and we're going to take our time and do it all. You do want to touch my breasts, right?"

He nodded but didn't move his hands.

Charlotte smiled. "Don't be shy, you won't hurt them." She caught his hands and brought them up to her breasts. "That's the way, Rob. You're going to do just fine, just fine." She reached up and kissed his cheek.

An hour later they lay on the bed. He hadn't said a dozen words as they made love slowly, deliciously. It was a training session and Charlotte was an excellent teacher. He made a move to sit up.

"Darling Rob, we're just getting started. We have all the rest of the afternoon to play here on the bed."

That afternoon Charlotte taught Rob all she knew about making love. Rob was a good student.

When Walter Albers came home from the bank that evening, precisely at 5:30 the way he did every weekday, Charlotte had his favorite dinner ready for him: a medium rare steak, baked potato, peas and carrots, and broccoli in a cheese sauce. There was a warm apple pie for dessert with a bowl of fresh whipped cream.

Charlotte's face was still flushed when she

reached up to kiss him when he stepped in the door.

Walter looked at his wife, saw her flushed face, the fluid, sexy way she walked and he shook his head. "Again, Charlotte?"

"I don't understand what you mean."

"You understand perfectly well. You took a man this afternoon. Here, in the hotel, or maybe even in this house. Somewhere. How can you go on humiliating me?"

"That's not true, Walter. Now please have your dinner before the steak gets cold."

He ate with relish because he loved a good steak and a good dinner. After it was gone he watched her again.

"Did you have him here in my own bed?"

Charlotte smiled. She had fulfilled her wifely duties with the house, with a good dinner, but he could not do his man's job.

"Yes, dear husband, I did. Your bed might just as well be used for something besides sleeping."

He tried to hit her but she jumped out of the way.

"I thought maybe getting you jealous would help you get it up, old man. Was I wrong? Can you get it hard for me right now the way you used to?"

Tears seeped out of his eyes. Slowly Walter Albers shook his head and turned away.

"I didn't think so. I'll leave the dishes for you, I'm going out. There's a poker game down at the hotel tonight. You don't need to wait up for me. I'll be home late."

Charlotte hadn't meant to rub the hatred in so deeply, but when he became so defeated that way, she just couldn't stop. She went to her bedroom and changed clothes. The dress she wore was cut low with thin straps over the shoulders. She had found that a flash of breast could unsettle a good poker player better than filling in an inside straight.

She added a touch more of rouge and lip color, then checked herself in the mirror. She stopped and pinned up her long brown hair until it had just the right flossy, wanton look. Then she walked the two blocks to the Prairie Hotel, nodded at Charlie the clerk, and went into room 12 on the first floor. She didn't knock.

Five men looked through the haze of cigar smoke at the door, then as one they stood, the game put on hold.

"Charlotte! Good to see you!" a small pot-bellied and balding man said. He was the meat market owner.

"Hope you brought your money along," Gus said. He was forty, a rancher who loved poker as much as an easy winter.

"Charlotte always bring her gold. I just hope she left her luck at home this time." The speaker now was Larry who ran the livery and owned two other buildings in town.

Two other men nodded and then all sat down when Charlotte did. She said hello to each man by name, then took two twenty dollar gold pieces from her purse and looked at Gus for chips.

"Table stakes," Gus said.

"Right, I know the rules. We can bet with only what we have on the table. I'm a regular here, remember?"

They played poker. Charlotte had learned to play with her crippled father and her two brothers. When the boys grew up the games went far into the night. They played only for matches then, but the thrill of winning and getting to razz the loser the whole next day made winning tremendously important.

Charlotte learned the odds in poker early and could bluff with the best in the business. She also used her womanly charms to fluster and confuse players when it would work. If she had to, she was sure she could make a living as a professional gambler going from town to town.

The first hand she lost. It was a ritual with her. She had learned from her father never to join a going game and win the first hand you're in. Bet short and fold. Then on the second hand you could start playing poker.

Charlotte won the second pot of seven dollars. They had a five dollar limit on bets because they wanted the game to last longer. Nobody could come into the friendly game with more than $40. That was still $240 on the table and made for a lot of interesting nights.

The makeup of the game varied from Tuesday to Tuesday, but more often than not, Charlotte played. After her wonderful fling with Rob that afternoon she had almost forgotten about tonight.

After an hour, Charlotte's stack of chips was down to ten dollars. Then her eye, her sense of the cards sharpened. She played lean and mean, checking the down cards, the showing cards, watching the men's faces critically.

In half an hour she had won three small pots and was back up almost even. Then Gus, the rancher, went on a winning tear. He took six pots in a row and had most of the chips on the table stacked in front of him.

The next game he called as he dealt was seven card stud, a game that took more chips and built up bigger pots. Charlotte had twelve dollars left. She looked at her two hole cards, an Ace and a King, both diamonds. Damn! The dealer laid out the cards around the circle face up. The last card to the dealer was a deuce and Charlotte's King of Clubs held up as high.

She knew a pair of Kings in seven-card wasn't much of a hand. She bet a dollar and nobody raised. The cards went down again. The deuce paired up and she caught a Queen — of Diamonds. Then Gus, the dealer, bet two dollars on his pair of deuces and she stayed in. She was down to nine dollars.

On the next face-up card she picked up a Jack of Diamonds. She was showing a Jack and Queen of Diamonds and a King of Clubs. Her two hole cards were an Ace and King of Diamonds. She was one card away from a Royal Flush, the best hand in poker! She had two more cards to get it.

Gus paused looking at her trio showing, grinned and turned over a deuce for himself. He was showing three of a kind.

"Gus, you're unconscious tonight," Larry said. Somebody else offered to step outside with him and duke it out in the hall. But it was all in fun.

"Hey, when you're on a lucky streak, don't matter what you do, you win," Gus said. "Tonight might be my night."

He bet five dollars and everyone stayed in. Charlotte was down to four dollars on the table. She had more money in her purse but that wouldn't do. Table Stakes.

The cards came around, the other four were out of it as far as Charlotte was concerned. Even with a pair under nobody had better than three of a kind. No straights possible, one possible flush but that wouldn't beat a full house which Gus could have. She watched her card come and inwardly groaned but put on a bright little smile. It was an eight of clubs. No help for her straight or for her Royal Flush.

Gus dealt himself a nine of diamonds and Charlotte almost lost her poker face fake smile.

"There goes your full house," she said with a touch of bravado.

Gus groaned.

"Now that's what I'd call a poker face groan of pain," Larry said.

Gus was still high on the board. He looked at the four one dollar chips left in Charlotte's stack.

"Gonna cost everyone five dollars to see the last card," he said evenly.

Three of the others folded. Larry stayed in with an outside chance at filling a straight if he had the fourth card in his hand.

"Five?" Charlotte squeaked. "You know damn well I only have four."

"I always bet the last card for five dollars when I'm ahead on the table," Gus said with a grin. "Ask anybody."

The men around the table grinned and nodded.

"You just don't want to give me a fair chance," Charlotte sputtered. "I mean, it's fair, it's legal, but it's still not right, and it's not very gentlemanly."

"Hey, in this game we decided a long time ago to treat you like one of the boys," Gus said, his smile still broad, still half teasing her. "You lose your lady's prerogatives at the door. Now, of course, that don't mean you lose your great good looks and beautiful manners and fine ladylike qualities."

"All right, all right, stop treating me like a child. We said this is table stakes, right? Whatever is on the table is what we bet with."

The five men nodded, not sure what was coming. Charlotte stood up and slightly grim-faced turned around and sat down on the table on top of her four chips.

"I'm putting one more item on the table, and you might say the bidding is open."

Gus chuckled.

Larry frowned. "You mean you're putting. . . ." He stopped.

Charlotte took a deep breath. "This is just between the six of us, never to be breathed outside this room. What I'm putting on the table is what you see on the table. You might say it's up for auction. The highest bidder pays me the cash now, I play out the hand and the game and if I can't pay back whatever is bid, then the bidder gets what's on the table now."

"Your ass in his bed," Larry said with a grin.

"Yes," Charlotte said calmly, smiling now, over the first embarrassment, ready for the fun. "Or in your case, Larry, my little round bottom in your haymow."

Everyone laughed.

When they quieted, Charlotte lifted her brows. "Come on you guys, any bids? Don't tell me you haven't had ideas about what's on the table. I've seen the way you guys look at me sometimes. Not very nice. A woman can tell."

"Hell," Larry said. "Five dollars."

Gus snorted, "Fifteen."

Charlotte was enjoying it now. "Bid up, you guys. You'll probably never get a chance like this again, because I'll probably never get a hand like this again."

"Twenty dollars," the youngest man at the table said.

"Twenty-five," from Gus.

Larry counted his money. "Table stakes on the bidding?" he asked.

"Damn right!" Gus said. He could outbid anyone.

"Twenty-eight," Larry said.

"Twenty-nine," Gus said and looked around the table. Nobody else had that much money left.

Charlotte held out her hand to Larry who counted out the money in red, blue and white chips.

She slid back into her chair. "You understand this is a conditional sale. The item in question isn't yours yet, unless I can't pay you back at the end of the game."

"Understood," Gus said. He laughed. "Hell, just thinking about it is worth twice that much."

"A month's wages?" Charlotte asked. "Coo, I should go into business."

Gus sobered and looked at his cards. "Back to poker. I believe the bet was around to you, Charlotte. The tab was five dollars."

Charlotte looked at her cards again although she knew what they were and would forever remember this hand.

She put a five dollar chip into the pot and then added one. "Five and bump you five dollars more."

Gus sat back in surprise.

"Hey, if I lose I lose big, but I can also win big."

"I'm in," Gus said and tossed in a red chip. It was just between the two of them now.

He dealt the last card to Charlotte face down. She picked it up, put it on top of her other two hole cards and holding them close to her breasts shuffled them top to bottom twice. When she looked at the bottom card she saw the King. She looked at the next card, the Ace. She checked the last card. It was a lousy five of hearts.

She'd lost.

Gus put a five dollar chip in the pile. "I'm betting a fiver. Up to the lady who sat on the table."

Slowly Charlotte folded her hand and tossed it into the pot showing that she was beaten.

"Oh, yeah!" Gus said and swept the pot onto his side of the table and passed the deal to Larry.

They played for another half hour. But the fun was gone. Nobody won or lost much. Charlotte watched her stake shrink to fifteen dollars, then she won a small pot and got up to twenty-eight.

The men kept looking at her, then at their watches. At last Larry made the move. "It's a little after midnight. I got to get home or my old lady will skin me naked. I've lost enough for one night."

Gus looked at Charlotte. "Are you ready to end the game?"

"I'm down to twenty-four dollars."

"I know." He grinned. "Hell, you can owe me the five dollars. Forget all that silliness about bidding for, you know, what was on the table."

"No," she said to Gus. "Cash me in, Larry. Gus, you go and rent a room from Jack. These gentlemen will keep your . . . your bid for property, safe until you get back."

Gus stood and watched her. "You don't have to do this, you know."

"The hell I don't! A gambling debt is a matter of honor. I pay my gambling debts, and all five of you remember that. But if any of you mention this outside this room, I'll kill you. Fair enough?"

An hour later Gus and Charlotte lay in the bed with only a sheet over them. She snuggled against him and Gus bent down and kissed her cheek.

"Where in hell did you ever learn to do. . . ."

"It's not polite to ask, Gus. Not proper. Is the debt paid, or only half paid?"

Gus laughed. "You really like it, don't you? Not many women do." He touched her breasts and lifted his brows. "Yes, I think the gambling debt is paid in full. And this will never be mentioned outside of that room. We didn't agree not to talk about it in the room, of course."

She hit him in the shoulder with her fist.

"I was just kidding!"

They dressed and he walked with her to within half a block of her house. Gus waited in the darkness and watched to be sure she got inside safely.

Charlotte undressed and slipped into bed. It had been quite a day, quite a day indeed. Rob that afternoon. So eager and youthful and so fast and so many times! Then the wild idea of betting her little bottom in the poker game.

The look on those five men's faces when she made the offer had been worth whatever it had cost her. Since she enjoyed the love-making with Gus, she figured she had won all the way around.

Now, who else was there in this town who was strong and handsome and willing who might interest her? She thought again about the tall man who she had met at the hotel dining room. He would be interesting, but he simply wasn't possible. She could always hope.

6

An early morning traveler at Prairie City kicked on the Town Marshal's office door about eight o'clock. Marshal Powell was just firing up his morning coffee on the small cook stove in the back room and groused all the way to the front door.

Marshal Powell stared at the dusty, bearded young man with more curiosity than anger.

"What the hell you want this early in the morning?" the lawman asked, pushing the door open.

"Thought you might like to know there must have been an Indian massacre or something about ten miles north of town."

"Don't say?"

"I come down the north road from Dodge City and I seen these vultures."

"We don't have no vultures in Kansas. Must have been hook-nosed hawks. Big black birds, jagged wing tips?"

"Yeah, something like that. Leastwise I got up to them and they took off and then I seen the damn bodies. Humans, all men. Six in a bunch and then five more strung out."

He handed the marshal a whip.

"Got to know one of these right good. It's a bullwhip. Used one for a year yahooing a six team of bulls around as a freighter. Found that near the bodies. Lots of sign around. Must have been six or eight big freight wagons. Two dead steers and a horse, and tracks all over the place. Way I figure it is some freight train coming into town got set on and all the bullwhackers killed and somebody took off with the goods. Tracks went every which way for a while."

"Not my territory," Marshal Powell said. "Sheriff up in Dodge City probably will be interested, or the U.S. Marshal if'n you can find him."

The young man stared in surprise. "Look, eleven men got killed out there, murdered, and their goods taken. Ain't you gonna do something? Ain't you a lawman?"

"Can't, not my jurisdiction. I'm the Town Marshal here. That's all. I got no say so outside the town limits." Marshal Powell shrugged. "If'n it looks like you say it looks like, it could be Injuns. If it is the work of the Comanche or the Kiowas from the reservation, then it's army business and they'll most likely want to know so they can handle it."

"By Damn! Here eleven men done been murdered outside your town and you don' pay no mind. What's the state of Kansas coming to?" He held up his hands when the Marshal waved one hand and started to speak.

"I know, not your jurisdiction. By damn, I'll go tell the army."

By the time the young traveler got to the army fort, it had started to rain. The thunderheads had been building up since daylight and the old hands around the plains got everything they didn't want to get wet in out of the weather. Now with the hint of heat at nine that morning the clouds tumbled over, lightning crackled across the land and thunder rolled. The clouds gushed down a hard driving rain that could produce an inch in an hour if it kept at it.

Colt had been in the Fort Commander's office when the young traveler came in. The civilian told his story again and Colt listened.

"Which direction did the tracks lead?" Colt asked.

"Generally south. From the position of the dead steers I'd say that was the way they'd been going when they were attacked."

"You find any Indian sign? Any arrows, knives, tomahawks, feathers, anything that might indicate that it was Indians who attacked the wagons?"

The young man furrowed his brow for a moment, then shook his head. "No sir. I seen Injun work before. Nobody was scalped, the bodies weren't mutilated at all. Ones I checked was shot to death, I'd wager."

Colt looked outside, then walked to the window. "Raining bucketsful out there. By the time we mounted up and rode ten, twelve miles out there, a Sioux tracker couldn't tell where those wagons went. The rain will wash them tracks out to a fair the well."

They excused the civilian who was given special thanks by Colt. He arranged for the man to dry off in the barracks and have dinner in the officers' mess before he resumed his journey.

Once he was out of the office, Colt looked at the map of the area spread across one wall.

"Ten miles up the north road would put them about, here." He pointed to a spot on the map. "To the left and south is Prairie City. Due south is the Comanche–Kiowa reservation."

Colonel Mason slumped in his chair and snorted. "Already you're jumping on the idea that old Saterlee bushwhacked some wagons that were most likely headed for his own Agency." He shrugged. "Hell, you might be right. With Saterlee, anything is possible."

"You get any notice by army courier when a wagon train of freighters is coming this way for the Agency?"

"Hell, no. Doing good to let me know what kind of Indian war we're supposed to be fighting."

Colt headed for the door. "Such a damn nice day, I think I'll mount up my men and go for a ride. Want to come along, Colonel?"

"Hell, no! Last time I rode a horse twenty miles I near died. Throw in the rain and I'd be dead before I got there. You go and enjoy yourself."

Twenty minutes later Colt headed out through the gate moving north with Sergeant Dunwoody and his six troopers.

Dunwoody spurred up beside the light colonel.

"Sir, we going on a training ride?"

"Not a chance, Sergeant. A traveler found eleven bodies ten miles up the north trail toward Dodge. He thinks they were bullwhackers and that somebody ambushed their train and made off with the wagons, freight and everything."

"That's why we brought shovels," Sgt.

Dunwoody said grimly. "Gonna be damn near impossible to track them vehicles after this rain."

"We'll try. With luck we might get a pointing."

They rode in silence after that. The men were covered with the only rain gear they had, their hats and an extra blue shirt. They were wet to the skin within ten minutes.

Colt settled into the McClelland saddle and gritted it out.

"Once you really get wet, a little more rainwater doesn't bother so much," Colt told the sergeant.

The series of pounding thunderstorms blew off to the east a half hour later and the sun came out. The men peeled out of their blue shirts and tied them behind them, then began to dry out.

Colt picked up the pace to a canter, jolting some of the men, but moving along at an easy pace for the horses and grinding out seven miles to the hour. They arrived at the site well before noon.

It was easy to find. A swarm of carrion eaters had descended on the bodies and were already picking at the faces and at any wounds that were available. Colt sent a rifle shot among the birds from a quarter of a mile off and sent them flapping away.

Colt walked the site and studied what was left of the tracks. The in-line deep ruts of the wagons had been left plainly in the soft ground even after the soaking rain. The heavily laden freighters could cut up a normal trail with one pass and cause rough problems for carriages and lighter rigs.

He charted the bodies, noting that one was well away from the others. Systematically he had the men go through the pockets and take out any personal effects, rings, watches, letters and keep them together. When that was all gathered, the men began digging graves off the trail.

"Three feet deep will have to do," Colt instructed.

He didn't even have names for some of the men. They would be a few more to join the great army of men who went West and vanished, never to be heard from again, leaving loved ones heartsick and never knowing what happened to them.

The troopers had cold rations at midday, then finished filling in the graves and put up wooden markers from brush they found nearby.

Then Colt called the troopers together. "We think these men were bullwhackers and that a number of wagons, perhaps as many as ten, have been stolen, along with all the goods. I'd like to find out where they went. They were heading south, maybe they kept on going. Let's spread out and look for soft spots where we might find some of the heavy tracks."

They spread out ten yards apart and rode in a half mile arc to the south. Before they had completed half of the circle, they came on three different spots where heavy wagons had crossed soft spots. Even with the rain the wheel ruts were evident.

Colt's tracker, a man named Philburn, took a sighting and they rode along in that direction for two miles and found another soft spot. Now it seemed that all the wagons had been on the same trail. It was off the main North Road and the ruts were deep where they showed.

A half mile before they came to the reservation markers, they found more of the wagon tracks.

Philburn came up and saluted.

"Sir, I'd say the wagons are now on the reservation. Can't be sure, but all the indications are they crossed about at this point and are now inside."

"Thanks, Philburn."

The young trooper saluted again and rode back to his sergeant.

Colt called up Dunwoody and they talked

as they rode back toward town. They were some four miles from the village and Colt eyed the terrain as they moved. A mile from the town he found what he wanted. A small creek came out of the plains and angled toward the Cimarron. A half dozen trees and a scattering of brush had grown up on a wide curve beside the little stream.

"Sergeant, I want you to take three men and set up an observation post in those trees. You'll be on twenty-four hour duty. I want you out of sight at all times."

"Yes, sir. I know the men I need."

"I'll take the other three back to camp and they'll return after darkness with supplies. That'll give you three men to be awake at all times. Nights will be most critical."

"You're expecting one or more of those wagons to come to town?" Sergeant Dunwoody asked.

"I'd bet on it, Sergeant. Sooner or later, Saterlee is going to want to start turning a profit on his haul. I'll be back tomorrow night. If you see a wagon coming from the reservation, take one man and follow it but stay out of sight. Determine exactly where it goes and where it unloads. Don't interfere."

"Yes sir."

"Move out, Sergeant Dunwoody."

Back at Fort Larson, Colt turned over the

personal effects of the civilians to the Base Commander who sent them on to the Town Marshal. He would forward them to the County Sheriff.

Then Colt told Colonel Mason what he had found.

"No sign of Indians, then?"

"Afraid not, but that doesn't mean they weren't there."

"But you know that means we can't take charge of the affair. Damn smart of somebody. If you could have found one damn Indian feather or a broken arrow we could move on it, charge right into the reservation in force, the way General Sherman directed."

"I've got an outpost watching the trail from the reservation. Oh, do you have a Gatling gun?"

"Two or three. Not a lot of call for them. Why?"

"I might want one, one of these days. Is it the kind mounted on artillery wheels?"

"Got one like that."

"Good."

Colt grinned at the bird colonel, popped him a perfect salute which the colonel didn't bother to return, and walked back to his quarters.

He set up the other three men with a pair

of pack mules and drew enough rations for seven men for a week, mostly hardtack and salt pork, but he also put in a sack of dry beans and a slab of good bacon. At the sutler's store he found some dried apples and prunes and he bought them with his own money and included them in the rations.

He had the three troopers get some sleep in the afternoon and just at dusk he started them on their way to the outpost. A corporal was put in charge and he rode across the plains with the two pack mules eager for a new assignment.

Now there was nothing Colt could do but wait. He put on his civilian clothes and prowled the stores still open in Prairie City, then had a beer in one of the saloons and listened to the talk. There wasn't much interesting, and nothing about the raid on the wagon train.

At last he joined a small stakes poker game and lost two dollars on the dime limit table. Still he had heard nothing about the wagons. He was back in his bunk before midnight.

The next day Colt rode to the outpost, coming at it from the north. He could see no one as he came up, and saw no smoke, but as he got closer he could smell smoke.

He pulled into the brush and a private was

on hand at once to take his horse. The men had built a well concealed little nest in the brush and trees. They had a small cook fire with beans simmering over the coals. Blankets had been rolled up neatly and the horses were a dozen yards away out of sight in the brush grazing on some spring grass.

Sgt. Dunwoody came to the officer at once.

"Didn't see a thing last night except one lone rider. He came from the direction of Prairie City. He headed for the reservation but can't say if he went there."

"When did he come back?"

"About two hours later. He was the same man and the same horse. We got close enough to tell. But he didn't carry nothing either way. Not a clue what he was doing, sir."

"Messenger, maybe. We'll see what happens tonight. I'll be here. How were the apples?"

"Going to cook some into sauce, sir. It'll be a nice change."

That afternoon Colt taught them how to build a snare and to bait the area. Most of the men slept during the day. Night was duty time.

It was just after two A.M. in the darkest part of the night when they heard something coming. Sergeant Dunwoody sent out a walking scout to see what it was and he came back quickly.

"Big Studebaker freight wagon and a team of twelve steers!" he told Dunwoody and Colt. "They just mogging along. Some guy dressed in regular civilian clothes has a big bull whip he slaps them with now and then. Must be a ton of stuff on that wagon?"

"More like two ton," Colt said.

"She's headed almost for us," the private said.

Twenty minutes later they could see the teams and the big wagon. It forded the small creek twenty yards from the brush at a rocky stretch, made it with no problem, and rolled along toward town.

Colt pointed to a corporal. "Get your horse and mine saddled up, we'll take a ride and see where this guy is going."

It was a slow ride. The big wagon creaked along at three miles an hour and it was nearly three A.M. before they came to Prairie City. The big wagon drove in along a short street past only two houses, and then turned down the alley behind Main Street.

It stopped at a store without any sign on the back. Before the bullwhacker could go to the door, a man stepped from the shadows and called and they talked a moment. Then the store man and the bullwhacker began unloading the wagon.

Colt and Corporal Warnick sat and waited. It took them more than an hour, then the wagon was empty and the bullwhacker moved the big rig out of town and headed toward the outpost and the Indian Agency.

Most of the goods had been carried into the back room of the store, but not all of them. The storeman was exhausted as he at last swung the door closed. They heard a bolt drop in place.

Colt and the corporal ran to the small loading dock and looked at the goods that were left. There were two coils of heavy chain, a hand plow, sacks that had labels that said they were seed corn, and a pile of other goods. Evidently the foodstuffs had all been taken inside.

Over the door a poorly hand lettered sign read: "J. A. Overbay General Store."

Colt grunted. So those used goods inside probably had been stolen. They heard the door bolt pulled and the two soldiers ran into the darkness and out of sight. The store man, who Colt now recognized as Overbay himself, came back with a big dog and chain. He fastened the chain to the plow and told the dog not to let anyone near the goods.

Colt and Corporal Warnick walked back out the alley to where they had left their mounts and hit the leather. They caught up with the big wagon a half mile out of town. It moved faster now, but not much. It seemed to be going back the way it had come, toward the reservation.

Back at the outpost, Colt assigned Dunwoody and another private to follow the wagon and see for sure where it went.

"If it goes into the reservation, make some kind of a mark where it enters so you can find it again. Pile three rocks on top of each other or take some sticks and push them into the ground in a pattern. Just so we know for sure where the wagon went back into the reservation."

Colt relaxed and had a cup full of the baked beans from the pot that still bubbled over a low fire. They were seasoned with some of the bacon and were the best he had eaten in years. Partly it was because he was hungry. At last he stretched out on his blanket.

He was putting the pieces of the puzzle together. Now he was sure Saterlee was behind the massacre of the bullwhackers. All he had to do was prove it.

When Sergeant Dunwoody came back from the reservation about four A.M. he had a curious report.

"Yes sir, the wagon went into the reservation. We marked it by driving four sticks into the ground in a pointing line. Then we were just about to leave when a white man came running out of the place. He looked wild and confused even in the moonlight. He had a full beard and had lost his hat. His hair looked to be uncut for a long time and stringy.

"He charged back into the reservation and came out with a horse. He rode right for us, came within ten feet of me. When he passed us he didn't even bother to look at us. I'm sure he knew we were there. Down one of his pants legs we could see a dark stain and there was red blood still on his hand and arm. Looked like a murder sure as shootin' to me, sir."

Colt scowled. "Damn strange. We saw a white man ride out of there two nights ago when we tracked the wagons, remember? Was it the same man?"

Dunwoody rubbed his face with one hand. "Can't say for sure, sir, but it was the same damned horse, I could swear to that!"

"Thanks, Sergeant, I'll put that in my report. Things are all over for tonight. Have some beans, or get some sleep. I can vouch for the beans."

The white man leaving the reservation worried Colt. The man surely wasn't Indian Agent Saterlee. Who was he and what was he doing inside the reservation? More important, was that human blood on his arm and leg?

7

Hirum Saterlee sat on a folding chair beside one of the big Studebaker freight wagons and surveyed his wealth. If he had been anywhere near St. Louis or even Kansas City, he could have ten thousand dollars in his pocket within a week.

Stuck out here in the middle of the prairie, the market was much more limited. So he would make the money over a longer period of time, no real problem. Overbay would be his major outlet. Actually, he would be the only outlet for the stolen goods.

Overbay said he'd take another wagon full in two or three days. Saterlee had unloaded half of one wagon there in the hidden draw where the wagons were parked so he could group all of the farm machinery and tools on one of the big Studebakers. In the other one he loaded the sacks of beans, corn, wheat and flour. There were barrels of salt pork, and while the farmers and ranchers didn't like it, there was a lively market for it among the town people who had no freshly grown meat supply.

Twice he had been over his remaining nine wagons of goods. He had pulled the army blankets and cooking equipment destined for the Indians into a separate place. They would get it eventually. The food was another matter. It could easily be converted into cash.

Short Knife appeared suddenly around the wagon and stood in front of Saterlee when the agent looked up.

"Damn yee, Short Knife, don't do that. Let me know you're coming. Scrape your feet or clear your throat or something. I could have shot you dead."

"You won't shoot me. I run the reservation for you. Without me the warriors would pick your bones clean. I need a sack of beans. My people decided they like beans."

"Half a sack. I can sell a whole sack of dry beans for five dollars."

"No, a whole sack. You owe me much more."

"Now just a minute, you —" Saterlee stopped quickly. He had almost ruined everything. He had no doubts that the young Indian in front of him would slit his throat in a moment if he became angry enough.

"Yes, take a sack of beans and use them well. Be sure your men keep the rest of the Indians away from this place."

"It is safe as long as I am safe," Short Knife said. He smiled, picked up a twenty pound sack of dry beans and hurried back to his camp.

Saterlee sighed. He watched the two braves move the last of the farm equipment. He would have that hauled down to the agency and he would try to teach the Comanche and Kiowa to farm, but he knew it would be a useless effort. Neither would dig up *Mother Earth's hair* by plowing. There was not a chance they would ever learn to be farmers.

Colt spent the rest of the day in the fort trying to figure out his next move. At last he decided he must wait for another wagon to be sent to the store. Then he would pounce on them in the act and have solid evidence.

He dressed in his civilian clothes and rode back into town and bought a new comb and pair of small scissors to trim his moustache. He made the purchase at the General Store and saw Overbay but didn't talk to him. Colt looked around the store but could find none of the stolen goods. At least he couldn't be sure. How can you identify beans and potatoes once they are out of the sack?

Colt walked the short three blocks of

Main Street on both sides. He found a few little stores he had noticed before, but none of them would be in a position to utilize the goods stolen from the wagon freight train. The General Store had to be the main, and perhaps the only, benefactor. The hardware store was a chance, but Overbay wouldn't want Saterlee to sell to him too, since on lots of items they were in competition.

Now all he had to do was catch Overbay in the act of receiving stolen goods.

Slowly, Colt realized someone walked beside him. He looked over and saw the woman from the restaurant, the proper "lady" who was really a whore at heart and in practice.

"Thought that was you," she said, glancing at him from huge brown eyes and flashing a beautiful smile. "Mind some company?"

"Always pleasant to walk beside a beautiful woman," Colt said without a smile.

"Why, thank you! Maybe you and I could have a small party after all."

"Not likely. Your husband wouldn't approve."

"Don't worry about Walter, he's not invited."

She tried to hook her arm through his, at last settled for holding his arm. He gently disengaged her hand.

Charlotte Albers frowned. "Oh, yes, I see. You don't want to be seen in public with me. Fine. Meet me at the hotel, room twelve, in fifteen minutes."

"What if room twelve is already rented?"

"It isn't. I have an arrangement with the management."

"That I can understand." Colt stopped. "Mrs. Albers, I'm just not interested in your suggestion. Why can't you accept that?"

"Nobody likes to get turned down," she said.

"First time for everything."

"I guess, and you are the first." She lifted her brows. "Well, I guess that is that. I'll be sure not to take up your valuable time again."

Colt touched his fingers to the brim of his civilian low-crowned tan hat, turned and walked the other way.

Slade Rogers stood in the front of the Prairie City Hardware watching Mrs. Albers on the boardwalk. Slade had combed down his wild hair the way his boss, Mr. Miller, told him to. But he had not been asked to cut it or shave off his beard. He looked a little less wild now than when he wasn't working.

He stared in open admiration at the sleek figure of the woman. It had been more than a year since he'd even thought about a woman. His wife, Julie, was still so close to him. But now he nodded. Charlotte was a real beauty, and he and everyone else in town knew that she would go to bed with almost anyone. She had never asked him, but then she didn't come into the hardware store often.

For a moment Slade thought of his wife and the great times they had in bed after the kids went to sleep. He ached with the memory and the pain almost began in his head, but he shook his head twice and drove the pain away.

He watched Charlotte again as she talked to a tall stranger. At last he said something to her and turned and walked away. For just a moment, Slade wondered what Charlotte would look like all warm and naked on his bed. Then he pursed his lips and firmed his jaw. Work. He had to work and learn all he could about the hardware business. He was never going to be a farmer again.

Well down the street from his confrontation with Charlotte, Colt stopped in for a civilian haircut, asking the barber to trim it up a little shorter than usual and to straighten up his moustache. Colt relaxed for a moment. This was one place a man could get fussed over a little and at the same time let down his guard. When the barber was done, Colt asked for a dash of the bay rum aftershave and grinned at the spicy fragrance.

Outside Colt headed for his horse and the mile ride back to the fort. He would get some new supplies for his team, the best food he could find, and head out for the nightly watch. Never could tell when Saterlee would try to run two or three wagons into the store.

When he had been there earlier today, he tried to come up with a good reason for getting in the back storage area, but Colt couldn't think of one that wouldn't make Overbay suspicious.

At the quartermaster he picked up eight steaks destined for the officers' mess from a freshly slaughtered trio of steers. He found some potatoes and some hard rolls that had been baked for the officers, and hurried to the outpost with his treasures.

Sergeant Dunwoody grinned when he saw the steaks. He let the men use the small cooking fire one at a time to fry their steaks in a frying pan they had brought.

The snare had produced one rabbit, but it had been eaten the day before. Any kind of fresh meat was a treat for the enlisted men, especially steaks, which never were served them, not even on Christmas or Thanksgiving.

Colt took his turn last on the fire frying his steak. He built up the fire a little and seared the beef on both sides leaving the middle blood raw. This was the only civilized way to cook a steak he told Sergeant Dunwoody.

Colt curled up on his blankets and told the men to wake him for the midnight watch.

Nothing moved past their post that night.

The next morning Colt and Sergeant Dunwoody scouted out a new outpost. They wanted one where they could see the reservation, so they could swear that the loaded wagon came directly from the Comanche–Kiowa lands.

By noon they had found a smaller version of their current place. It was adequate, had water and enough brush to hide them, but no large trees. They moved up to the new place just after dark. Now they were about three miles from Prairie City and a quarter of a mile to the reservation.

"Now we wait," Colt told the men.

Indian Agent Hirum Saterlee had picked up his mail himself at the drug store. The store was a contract station for the U.S. Post Office. They collected the incoming mail from the stage every day and sorted it and held it in alphabetical order for the people and businesses in town who came by and asked if they had any mail.

Saterlee had taken the two official envelopes with him back to his Agency. He pushed aside a letter from his wife and tore open the big Agency envelope.

It contained the usual hogwash, the rules and regulations and all the drivel that the Agency people came up with. He ignored most of it.

On a smaller envelope in the larger one he saw his name written in a careful hand. The finance man! He opened the small envelope carefully and his eyes shone.

There was a bank draft good for five thousand dollars! He read the letter that came with the draft with great interest.

"Dear Agent Saterlee: Please find enclosed a bank draft for five thousand dollars. These are specifically designated funds to be used for purchasing locally, at the prevailing price, beef cattle to be distributed to the members of your Agency. You are authorized for use of the funds as the need arises so the cattle may be bought in small lots for immediate use.

"Also enclosed is the authorization form and the required affidavits of purchase and bills of sale records that must be forwarded to this office not later than ten days following the last purchase."

Hirum smiled. Five thousand! All in one chunk! That was almost enough to tempt him to cash in and take off for California with a new name and a heavy bank book. No, not when he had another ten thousand worth of goods on those wagons. If he could get fifty cents on the dollar, that would make it five thousand more! Now a man could do a lot in San Francisco with ten thousand dollars!

A man could do a whole damn lot!

Patience. Another month. Could he hold off buying the beef for another month? No. Goddamnit, he couldn't. Some stinking congressional committee would come poking their noses about. He could buy half the beef, hold it, save the cash.

An idea began to germinate in his brain and he let it flower and grow. Two hundred and fifty head at twenty dollars would be five thousand. A hundred and twenty five, he could buy them for half the money. Then he might work out a deal with the rancher who sold them to the Agency to kick back half the money. No, too tough. Maybe he could get back half the money and let the rancher rustle the whole herd and sell them somewhere else?

Yes, that's it! Brilliant, absolutely brilliant. What rancher would work with him on this? Not the Bar-Bar. That guy was so honest he squeaked. Maybe Mike Guthrie. On the last beef buy they had arranged for the shipment to be shorted ten steers and the two of them split the profit in half on that one. How about the whole damn herd!

The Indian Agent danced a little jig around his quarters and grabbed Bright Night and swung her around, then caught her from behind and put his hands over her breasts and rubbed them.

"Now?" she asked. It was a new English word she had learned. She began to wriggle out of the soft squaw dress of fine chewed doeskin.

"No time, little pussy. Got to get out to see a rancher about a big deal."

He saddled up his horse and rode for town. At the bank he put half of the draft total in the Agency Account, and the other half into the Agency Beef account. He could get the money out at any time from either account. Walter Albers made out the deposit papers and Saterlee signed them, then hurried out to his horse.

It was a ten mile ride upstream on the Cimarron where it angled north deeper into Kansas to the Guthrie ranch. Saterlee didn't at all mind the ride. He had just made a cool two thousand five hundred dollars of clear profit! One damn stroke of the pen!

He was sure that Mike Guthrie would jump at a chance like this. He could sell the beef, and then later sell the same critters to the Agency again, or move them up state to the railroad and sell them the second time there. Who the hell was going to know the difference?

Saterlee kicked the horse into a canter, then a gallop for a quarter of a mile and eased off to a walk. Damn but he was excited. It wasn't every day he had a chance for a coup like this one. Damn but he was good!

8

Colt Harding spent two uncomfortable nights waiting in the darkness near the Comanche–Kiowa reservation, but no wagon came through. Neither did they see the white man on the skitterish horse who they had spotted twice before coming out of the Indian lands.

On the reservation, Saterlee continued to dig through his wagon loads of merchandise and supplies. He was amazed and delighted by the variety of goods sent by the government for the Indians. Most of it they had absolutely no use for.

He kept the food in a separate place and moved as much as he could to a guarded storage shed near his Agency house. Most of it would soon find its way into the civilian marketplace. He wished the town was larger! He thought of heading out to the surrounding towns with his wagons of wholesale goods to the stores, but he was afraid that would result in somebody asking too many questions about where he got the goods.

He waited anxiously for the third day after

he contacted the Guthrie ranch. The cattle would be driven into the eastern end of the reservation by Guthrie hands on that day. It was all arranged.

Saterlee met the cattle drive as the hands moved two hundred and fifty head into an open pasture at the far end of the reservation. Short Knife and twenty braves were on hand to help accept the beef. Saterlee had erected an eight foot square wall tent of pure white canvas on the site and brought in a folding table and two chairs.

When Mike Guthrie arrived he stared at the set-up and snorted.

"Looks like the surrender of General Thompson in the Civil War," he said. "All we're doing is selling you a few head of steers."

Saterlee motioned for him to sit down and took out a bottle of whiskey and two glasses. He poured three fingers of the amber fluid in each glass and lifted one.

"To good business," he said.

"Yeah, I'll drink to that."

They both drank.

"Everything just the way it was arranged?"

"Precisely, my good man. You deliver the two hundred and fifty head of steers to me. I pay you twenty dollars a head or five thou-

128

sand dollars and you give me a bill of sale. Then you 'rustle' the herd off the reservation. I keep four thousand of the money, you take a thousand dollars and you can sell the steers at the railroad or sell them to me again the same way in two months."

Guthrie finished off the whiskey. "You're the kind of man I like to do business with. But we could have just left the steers on my land and I brought you the damn receipt."

"Could have, but this way the Indians see the beef and can tell any investigator that the beef were delivered here on reservation land."

"Yeah, now I get it. Damn sneaky. But, hell, it's your money."

Guthrie took out a sheet of paper that had been written by a delicate feminine hand. He gave it to the Agency man. It was a bill of sale for the 250 head of steers at $20 each and had been signed by both Guthrie and his foreman.

Saterlee grinned, folded the paper and put it away in his jacket pocket. Then Saterlee took out from his other pocket a stack of new 20-dollar bills. He handed the stack to Guthrie.

"Fifty new bills there for you, Guthrie. Been a pleasure doing business with you."

Guthrie scratched the back of his head.

"Damn, you just made yourself a cool four thousand dollars."

"True, but you also made a thousand with no hassle and no worry. Most of all, you're taking no risk." He waved toward the open tent flap. "Now, I'd say our business is done, I'll bid you a good day."

They shook hands and walked outside. Once out of the tent, Saterlee gave a small hand motion and a rifle shot thundered into the quietness of the Kansas plains.

Guthrie ducked.

"Damn! That round almost hit me!" he thundered.

Short Knife laughed as he pointed a rifle at Guthrie from six feet away. "The next one will, Guthrie, unless you tell your cowboys to get off their horses and drop their six-guns on the ground," Short Knife ordered.

"What?" Guthrie turned to Saterlee. "What the hell is this? You cheating me, Saterlee, you bastard!"

"Short Knife, what are you doing?" Saterlee demanded. "Put the gun down. These gentlemen are here under my guarantee of safe conduct. We must let them return to the open range with their herd."

Short Knife laughed. "No. These white men violated Indian lands, we must defend ourselves, and save our cattle."

He spun to the left and fired the rifle. The bullet struck a cowboy who had drawn his six-gun in the shoulder as he sat on his horse. The blow of the round tumbled the cowboy off the mount and he sprawled in the grass holding his bloody left shoulder.

"No more gunplay!" Short Knife roared. "White-eyes, drop your weapons, now! Or I'll start shooting you out of your saddles."

One by one the cowboys dropped six-guns into the dirt.

Guthrie glared at Saterlee. "Control these savages! It's your job, goddamnit!"

"I'll try. But when they get like this. . . ."

"They're not supposed to have guns!" Guthrie shouted.

Short Knife motioned and more than a dozen Indian men ran forward and picked up the cowboys' weapons off the ground.

"Now your gun, Guthrie," Short Knife bellowed. "Put it on the ground, or I'll kill you."

"Christ! When you first told me about this deal, I should have known it was a sucker trap. Damn!"

"You have five seconds to live, Guthrie. One. . . ."

Guthrie lifted the six-gun out of leather and dropped it on the ground. "Goddamn,

Saterlee! I'll get you for this. Just wait. I'll see you hang!"

"Nothing I can do about it. I told them not to. Hell, you think I can control a thousand savages?"

"The money, Guthrie," Short Knife said. "Put the money on the ground, then walk away from it and get on your horse."

Guthrie held the stack of bills in his hand. "If I don't?"

"Then you're dead and scalped. Now you have another ten seconds to decide." Short Knife lifted the rifle and aimed at Guthrie's chest.

The rancher dropped the stack of bills beside his weapon.

"Go get on your horse and get out of here," Short Knife said softly.

Three Indians rode out of the brush, all on big horses, all with pistols on gunbelts and each carrying a rifle.

"Some of my men will be sure that you and your cowboys ride well away from the reservation," Short Knife said.

Guthrie looked at Saterlee. "You're a dead man if you step off this reservation!"

"I can't control these savages! I'm lucky to have lived so long out here. You want the damn job?"

Guthrie shook his head in disgust, walked

to where he had left his horse and stepped into the saddle. He watched a minute as six more mounted Indians rode up and began driving the cattle deeper into the reservation land.

Short Knife's three guards herded the white men off the reservation, then put half a dozen rounds over their heads to urge them to ride faster. The three men stayed near the boundary of the reservation, watching.

Back by the tent, Short Knife picked up the stack of bills and stared at them. "A thousand dollars! I've never seen so much money. I'm going to keep all of it."

"You agreed to drive Guthrie and his men off the reservation for half of it," Saterlee said. "You get five hundred, the other half is mine."

"That was before I saw how angry the white-eye was. He will cause trouble. I must have all of it now. You still made four thousand dollars today. Isn't that enough?"

"A hundred thousand wouldn't be enough," Saterlee said. He shrugged. "So keep it. We still have the goods to take to the store."

"From those I want half, not the ten percent you've been giving me. I can do sums. I'll bring the figures next trip from the store man. Half, Saterlee, I get half."

"All right. Go with the herd. Be sure that every tipi on the reservation eats fresh beef tonight, and makes jerky if the old women wish to. Make it a celebration."

Short Knife nodded and rode away on a pony another brave brought to him. In a short time he had become the most powerful man on the reservation. Powerful because he could bring food to the people's bellies. Now they had 250 of the white-eye's buffalo. By controlling them carefully in a small valley, they should last a long time and provide a continuing food supply for his people.

Short Knife grinned. He had no idea what the Kiowa would be eating.

When he left the reservation, Mike Guthrie swung wide, just out of sight of the Indian scouts, and headed for Fort Larson near Prairie City. He told his men to go back to the ranch and get their spare guns and rifles. He wasn't sure what they would do, but he wasn't going to let some slick politician steal five thousand dollars worth of cattle from him.

As he rode he worked out his story. He had contracted in good faith to sell two hundred and fifty head of cattle to the Agency. He had driven them near the reservation boundary, been paid and given a bill of sale. Then the Indians, with the help of the Indian Agent, had robbed him of the money and the beef and driven him and his men away from the reservation with rifle fire.

He would demand that the army launch an attack on the renegades who had returned to the reservation with the cattle and his money. He would scream so loud and long that the Army would *have to do something*.

Colt was talking to Colonel Mason in his office when the furious rancher stormed in.

"By damn! I been robbed by them Indians and their crooked Indian Agent, and I want the army to go in there and get my property back!"

They calmed the man down with a shot of whiskey, and then had him tell the story slowly from the start. He told it leaving out the part about going onto the reservation and about arranging for a kickback of the money and his getting to keep the steers.

Colonel Mason looked at Colt. "This is your bailiwick, Harding. What do you say?"

Colt stared at the rancher, who met his gaze for a moment, then looked away. "If what Mr. Guthrie here has told us is the absolute truth, then the army has cause to go in and straighten it out, reservation or no. You remember that General Will Sherman said the reservations were not a sanctuary where marauding Indians could plunder and loot and then return to be safe.

"Standing orders allow any Commanding Officer to pursue hostiles into a reservation and take any action required."

"So let's mount up five hundred men and go in there and get my beef back before them savages butcher them all!" Guthrie crowed.

"Not quite that easy," Colt said.

"How so? They stole my beef!"

"Did they? We have only your word on that, Mr. Guthrie. Is there any part of your story you want to change? We won't charge you with anything. We can't. We don't have any authority over you as a civilian."

Guthrie took a big breath and sighed. "Nope, that's how it happened. Exactly how it went. They stole my beef."

Colt walked around the room and looked back at Guthrie. "Then I'd guess my next job would be to take a squad of men and ride out to your ranch and question the men who rode with you today. Just to see if their stories were the same as yours."

"They'd all tell you the same thing."

"Are you sure?" Colt asked. "You don't seem quite as certain as you were a few minutes ago."

They looked at each other for a moment. Colt laughed softly and sat down across from Guthrie.

"If it's any help, Mr. Guthrie, I believe that Hirum Saterlee is a crook, a gouger, a con-man and a thief. He should be behind bars for twenty years. He's in a position to line his pockets with money and goods supposed to go into the hands of the Indians under his charge.

"It's easy for him to convert these goods and cash to his own uses. Like the beef buy. I'd be surprised if he agreed to buy beef from you on a straight, honest basis. Saterlee just doesn't work that way."

Guthrie tried to build a cigarette from paper and makings, but most of the tobacco fell to the floor.

"Mr. Guthrie, do you wish to change your story about the beef cattle?"

He shook his head.

"I'd be surprised if Saterlee didn't demand at least some of the money back from you that he paid you for the beef. He would probably want at least twenty-five percent of the total sale. Is that what happened?"

"Oh, damn!" Guthrie said. "You must know this bastard pretty well." He walked to the window, tried to light another smoke.

Colonel Mason gave him a thin black cigar and lit it for him.

"Mr. Guthrie, there's nothing we can do until we know exactly what happened out there," Colonel Mason said, using his most diplomatic tone. "Your crew will tell us if you won't. Why don't we get this all out in the open and then see what can be done?"

"Christ! What about what I done wrong? If I tell you everything, then you might arrest me, too."

Colt shook his head. "Mr. Guthrie, with Colonel Mason as your witness, I am hereby granting you immunity from prosecution for whatever happened out there on or near the reservation today with your crew and your herd of steers. You can tell us what went on and we won't charge you with a thing. We want to get Saterlee, and you can help us."

Guthrie nodded. "Yeah, okay, now I understand. Let me go over the whole thing from the beginning."

Six o'clock was closing time for the Prairie City Hardware, as it was for most of the retailing establishments in town, except on Saturday night when everything stayed open until ten to let the farmers and ranchers come to town and do the week's shopping.

Slade Rogers left by the front door, made sure it locked behind him, and headed across the street to Molly's for his one good meal of the day. Tonight was beef stew night and he loved the mixture of vegetables and big chunks of beef that Molly always put in her stew. It was more like fork food than stew, and he never missed Tuesday nights at Molly's restaurant.

He had just stepped up on the boardwalk across the street, when he saw someone at the inside of the sidewalk next to the wall of the law building. The couple seemed to be arguing and then Slade saw that a man had caught hold of the woman's arm and had pushed it against the wall so she couldn't move.

Slade frowned. No way to treat your woman, especially in public in broad daylight. He walked a step closer and he saw the woman was Charlotte Albers. Sure, he'd heard stories about her, and heard some men talk about how easy she was to get in bed, but he figured mostly it was brave talk.

She had always spoken nicely to him when she came into the store and twice he had waited on her. She was a lady.

"You did too go to the hotel with him, he told me so." The man's voice knifed through the suddenly quiet main street and people turned to watch.

Slade was the closest person to the pair. He was heading that way, to Molly's, and when he heard the woman raise her voice he walked faster.

"Get your hands off me!" Charlotte's strained, angry voice demanded.

Slade looked up in time to see the man grab at her dress front. She slapped him and he slapped her in return. By then, Slade had leaped across the six feet separating him from the couple and caught the big man's arm and spun him around away from Charlotte.

Only then did Slade realize the man was Big Harry Johnson, Prairie City's blacksmith. He was the strongest man in town and proved it every year at the Fourth of July parade.

"What the hell?" Big Harry growled. He saw Slade and snorted. "Skinny guy, you better go see your mama, I'm busy with this female."

Big Harry's one hand still held Charlotte's arm.

"Let her go, Harry," Slade said. "You're drunk. Go on over to Tessie's, she's got plenty of girls."

"Go to hell, Slade."

"Probably. When I get there I'll be sure to see you, Harry."

The blacksmith let go of Charlotte's arm and turned to face the much thinner man. Harry's arms and shoulders were like pile drivers, thick as an oak tree, bulging with muscles he used every day on the forge and anvil.

Slade had never been heavy, and at six-one he made a tall, skinny target.

Big Harry grunted and drove forward straight at Slade. The blacksmith looked like a buffalo charging. Slade had handled enough livestock to know the basics. Move quickly but at the last moment.

He did, sidestepping but thrusting out his right foot to kick Harry's near foot into his far one. The heavy man stumbled, crashed into the boardwalk and rolled off the edge into the dust and directly on a fresh cow pie an ox had just deposited before it moved a wagon out of town.

Harry jumped up, unmindful of the cow dung on his shirt.

Someone down the street guffawed. Harry looked that way with anger boiling out of his every pore. He jumped back on the boardwalk and angled for Slade, who had not moved.

This time Harry advanced slowly, deliberately, sure of his step, crowding Slade closer and closer to the wall.

"I'm gonna squeeze the shit out of you!" Harry bellowed.

Slade shot out a left jab. His fist landed on Harry's nose and blood squirted. Harry roared and drove forward, almost missing Slade as he jumped sideways but catching his left arm and dragging him back.

The blacksmith's huge arms circled Slade's back, ramming him against Harry's oversized chest. He began to squeeze. Slade had shot his arms upward to avoid the bands of human steel and now he pushed on Harry's chin, trying to bend his head back and break free. The arms tightened more and more.

Slade saw black spots in front of his eyes.

He couldn't breathe. Then he remembered a move a Chinese rail worker had told him about. It could injure a person severely, but it was better than being crushed to death.

Slade brought his hands up and clapped them together with his palms open. In between them lay Big Harry's head. Slade's open hands slammed hard against both of Harry's ears at the same time. For a moment there was no reaction.

Then Harry screamed a bellow of terrible

pain. He dropped Slade and put his massive hands to his head, shaking it, still howling like he had been run through with a rusty five-tined pitchfork.

Slade stood watching. Harry never looked at him. He kept screeching in pain as he staggered down the boardwalk for fifteen feet before plowing into the wall of the Overbay General Store and falling to the boards. He still touched his ears with careful hands and roared in pain.

Charlotte had waited a few feet away as the little drama had unfolded. Now she walked up to Slade and touched his shoulder. He turned to look at her.

"Mr. Rogers, I want to thank you for helping me. I didn't know what to do. I appreciate your help ever so much."

"Ma'am," Slade said, touching his fingers to his soft cap.

She was the prettiest woman he had ever seen. She watched him a moment, then turned and walked quickly the other way down the boardwalk toward her big house.

Slade watched her go, then angled past the still blubbering blacksmith and into Molly's Restaurant.

He sat at the counter and ordered the stew and a big cup of coffee.

A large woman with pillow sized breasts

pushed through the kitchen door and stared at Slade. She walked up to him across the counter and smiled.

"That was a mighty brave thing you just did, Slade Rogers."

He shrugged. "Just something that needed doing. I happened to be there."

" 'Deed you were." She grinned. "The dinner and a piece of cherry pie with some of that cold iced cream on it compliments of the cook. You eat your fill, you earned it."

9

Short Knife sat in his tipi in the reservation and slowly spread out the fifty paper money twenty-dollar bills. They were new ones, had never been used by anyone. They were beautiful!

They were wealth, riches that no Indian had ever known. With the other paper money and gold coins he had, he was truly a rich Indian. So what did he do with it? Should he leave the reservation and go to the white-eye's town and cut his hair and live as the whites lived?

Short Knife remembered how he had been treated even as a youth in the white-eye's town. No, he would not go there again to live. But he could taste some of its pleasures.

He collected the money, put it away in the hidden place under the edge of the tipi cover where it folded inside to keep out the winter winds. He had dug a small hole and put the metal box there for safekeeping. Not even his women knew about it.

Next, Short Knife put on his white-eye clothes — pants, shirt and belt. He found the boots he had stolen at one of the ranches and pushed his feet into them. Then he put on a cowboy hat and hid his long hair under it. He was ready.

Short Knife cut his war pony from the herd and rode quickly into Prairie City. He came in by the side road and the back streets and saw a few white-eyes walking around, but none had guns and none paid any attention to him. He was just another stranger riding into town.

Short Knife grinned as he rode into the alley behind Main Street. He had been to this small town many times, and no one had discovered he was an Indian. The bartenders were more careful and looked at him closely. The second time in town he had been run out of a saloon.

Now he found the rear door of a drinking establishment and tied up his horse. He waited for someone to come out the back door heading for the white-eye's outhouse. It was never a long wait near a saloon.

One man dressed in a black suit and string tie came out. He looked around, adjusted the six-gun tied low on his hip and stared at Short Knife for a moment, then evidently discounting him as a danger, went to the outhouse.

Short Knife laughed. "Nobody. Just bring

me back midday." He had all afternoon. The third man who came out staggered on his way to the relief station. He was drunk, but not too drunk.

Short Knife took a dollar bill from his pocket and when the drunk came back toward the saloon, he stopped the man.

"Hey, you want to make a dollar?" Short Knife asked.

The drunk looked up and tried to focus his eyes better, gave up and nodded. "Da. . . . damn right. Who I gotta kill?"

Short Knife laughed. "Nobody. Just bring me back a dollar bottle of whiskey. You bring it back and I'll give you another dollar. Understand that?"

Short Knife made him repeat the instructions before he gave him the paper note. Then the drunk nodded and wobbled toward the saloon door. As he stumbled through and inside, Short Knife wondered if he had picked a man who was too drunk.

About five minutes later the same drunk came reeling out the door, leaned against the side of the wall and started to open a bottle of whiskey.

Short Knife jumped to his side and pulled the bottle away from him. He took two quarters from his pocket and gave them to the man.

"Here's your dollar, four quarters. Now go and buy yourself twenty more beers."

The man thanked him three times, never bothered to count the quarters and struggled to open the door again, then he vanished inside.

Short Knife snorted, walked to the street and out to Main. He found some shade near the dry goods store and sat there in a tipped back captain's wooden chair and watched the people go by. From time to time he took a pull from the bottle, which he hid in the flowing folds of his shirt.

He enjoyed pretending to be a white-eye from time to time. And he could always get whiskey. Drink a little and watch, drink a little more.

As he thought about his visits to town over the past year, he remembered his one try at using a whore. It had been in one of the saloons, and the girl had been a little drunk herself. When they got upstairs in her room and she took off his hat and saw his long Indian black hair spill out, she took a good look at him, screamed, and ran out of the room.

He went down the outside of the building and ran through the alley before the shotgun man came up the stairs.

Now he just looked at the white women.

They were little different from his wives. He'd had enough naked white women lately on the raids to be sure of that.

After an hour of drinking and loafing he wandered down to the far end of the street and leaned against a store front. To his left he saw a new movement. A woman came down the side of the dirt street, her long skirt brushing the dust.

Something about the way she walked caught his attention. She held her head high, like a Chief, she moved smoothly and he could imagine the fluid motion of her hips under the dress.

When she came closer he saw she was a tall woman, with striking brown hair around her shoulders and a pretty face. He had never thought much about the looks of a woman before, but this one intrigued him.

Then she was in front of him, not ten feet away, and she looked him right in the eye. It was unusual for a white woman to look that way at a stranger. He stared back at her and he smiled. For a fleeting moment he saw a smile brighten her face, then she looked away and was past him. She went down three stores and walked inside the dress shop.

A few minutes later she came out and walked back toward him. Now he noticed her breasts, they were full and high. He didn't think he'd ever seen a bigger pair of tits. Not even on that young white girl he'd made love to when he was fifteen and living in the white-eye town.

She walked back his way and he waited. When she looked up and saw him, the woman changed her direction and walked toward him. She watched him as she moved. She had a broad, pretty smile as she stopped in front of him.

"That wall won't fall down, you don't have to hold it up anymore."

Short Knife laughed. Now that he could see her up close, he was more interested in her than ever.

"You're brave talking to a stranger."

"I do what I want to do." She looked at him again, saw the bottle inside his shirt. "I'm Charlotte Albers, what's your name?"

"Buck," he said automatically, using the white-eye name they had given him when he was fourteen.

"You must be a cowboy."

"Yes."

"Were you waiting for me?"

"Hoping."

"I came back wondering if you'd still be here. Would you like to see more of me?"

"I'd like to see all of you."

A quick blush touched her neck and face. She beat it down.

"Good." She hesitated. "You are a Comanche, aren't you? You must be Indian."

"Would it frighten you if I am Comanche?"

"No, that would make it exciting. I've never known an Indian before. Never had one in my bed." She smiled. "Does that shock you?"

"No, not if it's an invitation."

"It is. Your English is good. Don't follow me now, but come to the back door of the hotel to room twelve, in about ten minutes. No tricks. I'll be waiting for you." She moved a little closer. "Then you can do anything with me you want to and do it several times, I hope." She grinned, turned and walked back toward the hotel which was one block down on the corner.

Short Knife turned away from her as she left. He took another drink from the bottle and smiled. She was an interesting white-eye woman, one who didn't mind asking for what she wanted. She even knew he was Comanche. There was no decision to make. He would go and take the white woman. Then he would decide what to do with her.

Short Knife went around the block, came up through the alley behind the Plains

Hotel, and then slipped in the corner building's side door. Room twelve was two doors down the hall. No one else was in the passage. He started to knock, then turned the knob and pushed the panel open slowly.

Short Knife gasped, then stepped in and closed the door softly. The white-eye woman stood in front of him. The window blind was down and she stood waiting, naked, her breasts thrust outward, her stomach drawn in. He had never seen such a beautiful woman, or one who was so in need of a man.

He ran forward, caught her and eased her down on the bed. She insisted that he take off his clothes, and then he was beside her.

She shook her head. "An Indian man doesn't look any different to me than a white man. Tell me, is a white woman any different?"

"Only the ones who like to make love," he said.

"There aren't a hell of a lot like me," she said softly.

Short Knife smiled. "There probably isn't another one like you in the whole country," he said.

Then he took her, savagely.

She loved it.

The wife of the hotel owner, who cleaned the rented rooms, found the note about ten the next morning. She was getting the room ready for another renter when she saw the paper on the dresser. She was about to throw it away when she saw writing on it.

"Please! Tell my husband I've been kidnapped by Indians. They broke in last night while I was resting. They are Indians! They demand five thousand dollars ransom. It must be paid within two days or the Indians will torture me. Each day you don't pay, the price goes up by five thousand dollars, and the Indians will send a cut off part of my body to my husband. Please pay quickly!"

The note was signed "Charlotte."
There was only one woman or girl in Prairie City named Charlotte.
The woman showed the note to her husband, who took it at once to Town Marshal Powell. He went to talk to the banker, Walter Albers. By noon everyone in town knew about Mrs. Albers being kidnapped. Most figured she had it coming. The rest were surprised something like this hadn't happened before.

Marshal Powell looked at Walter Albers. "My suggestion is that you pay like it tells you to there on the bottom of the note. Take the money out to that old lightning-struck cottonwood and get your wife back."

"We've had our problems, Marshal, as I'm sure you know. But you're right. I can't just leave her out there? I've got to pay. Don't know as I've got that much cash in the vault."

"You get ready, I'll ride with you for the exchange. Least I can do, even though she's off my jurisdiction."

Walter Albers shook his head. "Get out of here, Marshal."

By one o'clock that afternoon, they knew about the abduction at the fort and Colt heard the news shortly afterwards. He quickly figured out the woman was the same one who had invited herself to his dinner table in the hotel.

"We could take two fully armed companies to go into that reservation and find her," Colonel Mason said. "But we don't have that many combat troops on the whole post. We'll let the civil law handle it."

"What about the sanctuary regulation by General Sherman?"

Colonel Mason shook his head. "In this case, I can't remember that regulation at all.

Hope to hell you can't either. We got ourselves trouble enough as it is."

Colt knew he was right. Still it rankled him. He rode out as usual for his watch at the outpost near the reservation. He took two freshly baked loaves of bread to the troops and a jar of jam he stole from the officers' mess.

Well fed troops are happy troops, Colt always said.

"You're spoiling us," Sergeant Dunwoody said as he cut off another slice of bread and smeared it with the strawberry jam.

"Part of my job," Colt said. "I've got you on special duty, that should involve special chow."

Colt took his usual nap from dark to midnight, then was up with the guard. They heard the creaking of a dry axle just after one o'clock that morning. Colt woke the rest of the men, and had them break camp and pack up all their gear. As the wagons came by, Colt saw that there were two of them. Each wagon was tended by a man in civilian clothes with a bullwhip. Whoever wielded the dangerous whips seemed to know what they were doing. Each of the big Studebaker wagons was pulled by a string of six pair of steers. One curious difference this time. An Indian pony with halter but no saddle had been tied to the rear of each wagon on a lead line.

"Looks like this time they won't be bringing back the wagons or the teams of steers," Colt said.

They were nearly four miles from town, and the plodding steers were unhappy about being rousted out of their sleep. They made little more than three miles to an hour.

When they came to town they took the same route as before, up a side street, then into the alley behind the J. A. Overbay General Store.

Colt put two of his men at the far end of the alley, stationed another one at the front door of the general store, and took the other four with him. They left their horses two blocks away and moved into the alley on foot, slipping up the near end of the passage until they could get a good view of the unloading in the half dozen lanterns that had been hung on the wooden dock.

This time there were three other men there taking goods off the wagons. The drivers simply sat and waited for ten minutes, then went up and one of them talked with Overbay. The merchant argued for a moment, then wrote out a paper and signed it and handed one of the two bullwhackers a heavy cloth sack. The two drivers in civilian clothes went at once to their horses.

One went out of the alley each way. The rider came toward Colt and his four men at the short end of the alley.

The four men stepped in front of the horse with pistols drawn. The rider swung off the side of his mount and charged forward. He hung on the side of the horse where Colt was. The officer held up the butt of his pistol and cracked it into the rider's head as he raced past.

The jolt drove the weapon from Colt's hand but also smashed the rider off the horse. He lay on the ground without moving as the horse kept galloping down the alley and turned at the street heading for the reservation.

"Tie him up," Colt whispered. He took Sergeant Dunwoody with him as they ran back toward the general store. At about that time gunfire blazed from the far end of the alley, and then a horse raced away.

Colt and Dunwoody ran up to the loading dock and Colt fired a round into the air. The three men on the dock looked up in surprise.

"You men are all in custody of the United States Army. Lace your fingers together on top of your heads and don't move."

The three men outside complied at once.

"What the hell's going on?" one of the men asked.

"This is stolen property you're unloading," Colt snapped.

He heard a commotion inside and soon the trooper who had been at the front door came out with his pistol pushing Overbay ahead of him.

"That's the last of them, Colonel," the trooper reported.

One of the men from the other end of the alley ran up.

"One of them got away. He spoke English and we weren't sure he was Indian. Then he knifed me in the shoulder and knocked me down and was gone. We fired but I don't think we hit him."

Colt studied the problem a minute. "Okay, load everything back on the wagon. Do it now."

The three men looked at Overbay. The merchant sighed and nodded. "Better do it. He caught us red-handed."

The troopers supervised the loading. One man bandaged up the trooper's knifed shoulder.

"Overbay, you and I need to have a nice long talk. You have an office?"

An hour later the loading was completed, but Colt still talked with Overbay.

"What this all comes down to, Mr. Overbay, is that you either cooperate with me or go to prison. It shouldn't be a hard choice to make."

"I still don't understand."

"You've admitted that you knew the goods were supposed to go to the Indian Agency. That makes them federal property. The penalty for theft of federal property is ten to twenty years in federal prison at Leavenworth. You accepted at least three loads of goods. I saw you take in all of them. That's grand larceny. I'm a good witness, Mr. Overbay."

"If I cooperate?" Overbay had loosened his shirt. He was sweating now, pacing the small office.

"You'll return all goods you bought from Saterlee. Every bit of it you haven't sold. You'll compensate the U.S. Government for any goods you sold. You will testify against Saterlee, telling the court exactly how he approached you, what he said, what he offered."

"That's all?"

"No, I'll guarantee to you that we won't prosecute you for your part in the crime, if you tell everything to the court. That means you can't be charged or tried on the theft charge and you won't go to prison."

Overbay sat down and mopped his fore-head with a big red handkerchief. "I don't have much choice, do I?"

"Mr. Overbay, you don't have any choice at all. We'll get it all down in writing to-night. Do you agree?"

The merchant nodded.

"Then first we go get those three men and have them start to sort out and stack on your dock all of the goods you got from Saterlee on that first load."

"That'll take some time."

"We've got all night. You start moving out the goods, and I'll write up an agree-ment for you to sign."

Colt talked to Sergeant Dunwoody. The man riding the war pony Colt had hit on the head turned out to be an Indian and he died of his head wound.

By four A.M. a second pile of food and merchandise had been stacked on the loading dock. The three civilians who did the loading were allowed to return to their homes. Each had sworn that he was hired simply to unload wagons, and that he had no knowledge that he was moving stolen goods. They would not be prosecuted.

Colt had written out the agreement to tes-tify against Saterlee with an assurance that Overbay would have immunity. A list of general actions by Saterlee was also spelled out. Overbay read it and signed it quickly. Then Colt signed. Sergeant Dunwoody witnessed both men signing the document. Then the merchant was sent home.

Colt and his men slept on the dock until morning. Then he rented a freight wagon from the livery and two teams of mules to pull it. He brought it to the Overbay dock and his men loaded it as Overbay, who had come back to open the store, watched.

By nine that morning Colt's men had the wagon loaded. Three bullwhackers had reported to the dock ready for work. The livery man had said he would send around three men for a day's work. The little wagon train made a small scene as it wound through the side streets of Prairie City and out toward the fort.

Colt had decided that he would keep the Indian Agency goods at the fort until the Saterlee affair was finished. Now he had two witnesses that Saterlee had committed felonies against the U.S. Government. A conviction should be quick and easy and Saterlee shunted off to Leavenworth for fifteen years.

The crack of the bullwhips sounded over the prairie as the drivers pushed the two steer-pulled wagons and the mule skinner urged his teams forward.

Colt felt as if he had put in a good day's work. The one nagging problem still concerned him. The woman. No white woman should be left in the clutches of Indians. But the word was that these Indians had actually asked for cash money. That was unusual.

Most Indians had no idea of the concept of money. They dealt in goods. A warrior's wealth lay in how many horses and mules he owned. A wife was paid for with a gift of horses to her father. What Indian was interested in cash money?

Perhaps, after the Saterlee affair was finished, he could look into the problem of Mrs. Albers.

Perhaps.

10

Colt left the three wagons of food and merchandise parked in the open at Fort Larson with a 24-hour guard established around them. Then Colt had his wounded trooper examined by the fort doctor and his wound treated and dressed.

Colt met with his five remaining soldiers. They all reported they were ready for duty. He mounted up the five men and rode for the reservation and the Indian Agency.

At the edge of the reservation where the trail entered, a crude gate had been erected from poles. It was only a frame in the air but to the Indians it was either the entrance to the worst or the best place on earth.

The gate was about a mile from the Agency Headquarters house. Colt walked his horses through the reservation until he could see the Agency house, then he called out that he had come to talk with Agent Saterlee.

Saterlee came bustling out the door and waved them forward. Colt was sure that Comanches had seen them coming and relayed the news to the Agent.

Saterlee stood by a small porch on the house as they rode up. He nodded to Colt, who stepped down and saluted him.

"Mr. Saterlee, Mr. Hirum Saterlee, Indian Agent for the Cimarron Comanche–Kiowa Reservation?"

"That is correct, Colonel."

"Lieutenant Colonel Colt Harding, sir. I would like to request a short conference with the Indian Agent."

Saterlee lit a long, expensive cigar he had become used to in Washington, and blew out a mouthful of smoke before he responded.

"Yes, I think we might arrange that. Come inside out of the dust and the flies."

At the door, Saterlee urged the enlisted men to come inside as well. Colt objected and told them to remain outside and keep their eyes open. The room had a desk with Saterlee's fancy nameplate on it and a U.S. flag. Saterlee sat down in a large upholstered chair behind the desk and waved at a hard oak chair beside his desk for Colt.

Colt remained standing.

"Agent Saterlee, I'm representing the United States Government by authority of General Philip Sheridan. As you must know, the two wagon loads of stolen merchandise you tried to sell to J. A. Overbay last night in Prairie City were intercepted and are now being held as evidence."

"I don't know what you're talking about, Harding," Saterlee said, but sweat had beaded his forehead.

"I'm sure you do. We have a deposition from J. A. Overbay about the complete series of meetings, talks, deliveries and payments that have been made so far between the two of you. He spoke of the ten wagon loads of goods sent to your Agency but bushwhacked on the trail. We know about the eleven men murdered, and the train diverted into this reservation. You then reported the train of goods stolen to your superiors.

"A Comanche Indian dressed as a white man was killed last night when he attempted to escape after driving one of the wagons from this reservation to the alley in back of the Overbay General Store."

"No skin off'n my nose. My Indians get into all sorts of trouble."

"The other driver got away with the payment, over a thousand dollars, according to Mr. Overbay. I'm putting through formal charges against you today, Mr. Saterlee, charging you with grand theft of Government property. Also you'll be charged with eleven counts of murder for the bullwhackers on that freight train.

"We have twice the evidence we need to convict you. A minimum sentence will be from twelve to twenty years and a twenty thousand dollar fine, for the theft. The penalty for murder, as you well know, Mr. Saterlee, is hanging."

"You've got shit for evidence," Saterlee said. "I haven't done a thing wrong. I never killed anyone. About the storekeeper, it's his word against mine. He had the goods. I never have had them. You can't tie me in with it at all."

"We can, Mr. Saterlee, and will. The second set of charges include defrauding the U.S. Government of five thousand dollars designated to be used to buy beef for your Agency's Indians."

"I don't know what you're talking about."

"I have a signed deposition from Michael Guthrie that you agreed to buy 250 head of steers from him at $20 a head. He states that you took delivery of the cattle and a signed receipt, then defrauded him of his pay, and by force of arms, drove him and his cowboys off the reservation and kept the cattle."

"He can't prove a thing, shyster. You're starting to sound like a crooked lawyer. What's your cut on all of this?"

"Satisfaction, Saterlee. The satisfaction

of seeing scoundrels and thieves and violators of the public trust, assholes like you, charged and convicted and sent to prison. That gives me just one hell of a lot of satisfaction."

Saterlee puffed on his cigar. "Soldier boy, you know who I am? You know the connections I have in Washington? Do you know that I can get ridiculous charges like these thrown out of any federal court you file them with?"

"Not a chance, Saterlee. The army has mighty good connections too, in Washington. We can prove each of these charges with up to ten witnesses on one and with three on the other. You have a loud voice, Saterlee. When you speak, people in the next room can hear you — and then swear to it in court."

"Let me call for one of my Comanche assistants. He can swear to where I was last night. I had nothing to do with that merchandise."

"No!" Colt spoke sharply. "I don't want you to call anyone. There will be no tricks and no accidents while we're on the reservation. You'll be riding with us to the edge of the Indian lands to insure that. I have given you official notice of the charges I'm going to file. My suggestion to you would be to confess to the lesser charges and hope that the court might dismiss the murder charges."

Colt shrugged. "I've seen a lot of these. You try to fight this one, and chances are nine out of ten that you'll hang." Colt smiled. "Now, get your hat, Indian Agent Saterlee. We're going for a little ride. You give any signal or advise your Indian friends to shoot at us, and you'll be ⸻ ⸻ ⸻ to die. Do you understand?"

"Bastard!" Saterlee ⸻ "I'm warning you, soldier boy, y⸻ ⸻ ⸻ the last about this. I'll show ⸻ ⸻ can fight."

On the way back to the fort, Colt tried to think what he would do now if he were in Saterlee's shoes. He'd com⸻ ⸻ ⸻ tight scrapes by applying th⸻ ⸻ ⸻ before. The whole case h⸻ ⸻ ⸻ nesses, and Saterlee knew who they were: Guthrie and Overbay.

Which one would he try to take out first?

Overbay. He was closer and had no protection around him.

Once the army detail arrived at the fort, Colt let the men take a break and have chow. He told them to relax, get some sleep, they would be up that night. Colt gave Sergeant Dunwoody specific instructions. Then Colt rode into town for a long talk with Overbay.

The merchant agreed to let his clerk keep the store going in the afternoon. He went home and had his wife go spend the night with a good friend three houses down. They had no children at home. Colt had spent the afternoon in the back of the store, waiting. He had worn both of his pearl handled pistols this time.

Nothing happened before closing. Colt left when the clerk closed the store for the night. At the hitching rail outside the bank he found Sergeant Dunwoody. Colt motioned to the man, who mounted, and the two rode down the street.

"Get the other men and as soon as it's dark, we move into Overbay's house. I'd bet my last dollar that Saterlee and some of his Indians will be making a house call tonight."

The troopers left their easily identified army mounts tied to hitching racks around town and assembled two blocks from the target house. Colt had no idea if Saterlee was watching the place, but if he was, he had seen Overbay twice in the two hours before it got dark.

The moment dusk closed in Colt and his men worked down the alley and into the back yard, then through the back door. Overbay knew they would be coming. He had laid out two rifles of his own and a shotgun that held two rounds.

"You really think he'll come after me?" Overbay asked. There was a trace of anger in his voice, but that was swallowed up by the raw fear showing through.

"He's a smart man, a politician used to playing the angles. He'll be here, or out at the ranch. I sent a rider out there this noon to warn them they should be ready for uninvited guests. My guess is he'll hit you first because you don't have twenty gun-toting cowboys bunking at your place."

Overbay looked around. "Glad I have the seven of you."

Colt positioned his men at strategic positions around the house. Sergeant Dunwoody went to the rear second floor window. He cracked it four inches so he could hear outside. He would be overall watchdog for the rear.

Another man sat near the front windows in the living room and the dining room. Colt was in the small woodshed that led into the kitchen through the back door. He guessed it would be a quick hit through the back.

Colt put Overbay on the second floor to keep him out of the way as much as possible. He told Overbay to push a mattress across the room's one window, lock the door, and place any heavy furniture in the room against the door.

"We won't be coming in there, so if somebody tries to force his way in, shoot and worry about who it is later."

Overbay nodded and handed Colt the shotgun. "You'll need this if they get this far."

He went upstairs and Colt heard him sliding furniture.

It had been dark less than five minutes when Colt had the house armed like a fort. Each of the troopers had his six-gun and a Spencer repeating carbine that held seven shots in the magazine tube and one loaded and locked in the chamber. Counting six rounds in the revolver, that was fourteen rounds without reloading. Should be enough.

If Saterlee brought reinforcements, they would be Indians. He had no friends in town that Colt had found.

They waited.

An hour dragged by. Colt made the rounds silently. A lamp burned in the living room. No fire was needed. Upstairs he cautioned Dunwoody to hold fast. He spoke to the other men, then returned to his post and waited.

Another hour came and went.

It was slightly before ten that evening when Colt sensed more than heard someone at the rear door. He lifted the shotgun and waited. There was no light in the woodshed, since it normally would be dark.

The rear door swung outward and now Colt saw it edging open a quarter of an inch at a time.

Indians. Had to be to have that much patience. Colt's eyes were accustomed to the little light that came from the living room through the kitchen and into the woodshed.

At last the door was open a foot. A hand touched the inside of the door and edged it open another two inches, then a body wearing civilian clothes slid sideways through the opening.

Had to be an Indian.

Wait.

Was there only one?

The form took a step inside, then squatted on the wooden floor. Another body filled the door behind him. Two of the bastards. This one also wore white man's clothes and a hat that concealed any long hair.

Colt waited. The first man moved three feet into the woodshed, kicked the chopping block, and whispered a word Colt couldn't recognize.

The third man sidled through the door, and Colt's fingers tightened on the shotgun's trigger. One pull for one barrel, another pull for the twin barrel. He'd made sure the rounds were double-ought buck: a dozen pellets the size of a .32 caliber slug in each cardboard shell.

"Go on, go on!" the third man in the door whispered.

Colt sat with his back against the side of the woodshed less than ten feet from the men. That was the team, three men.

"Freeze in place and live!" Colt barked.

One dove for the floor, the other two lifted weapons. Colt's trigger finger squeezed the first time. The shotgun's raging roar in the woodshed nearly deafened Colt. The twelve slugs ripped through the back of the man who dove to the floor and half of them splattered into the man who had crouched just behind him. The third man spun pushing toward the door.

Colt's finger pulled again and he lifted the muzzle four inches. The second blast thundered like a dynamite explosion in the contained room and the third man at the door caught all but one of the .32 caliber buckshot pellets and they blew him out the door into the back yard.

Colt's ears rang as he waited. He had dropped the shotgun and lifted both his six-guns waiting for some reaction.

He heard feet pounding the stairs and the living room.

"Hold your positions!" Colt bellowed. The movement stopped.

Deathly stillness shrouded the woodshed.

Then a voice gurgled. "God's sakes, help me!"

Colt waited. He had heard none of the men move.

"A lamp," Colt barked.

Someone brought a lamp to the kitchen door. Colt never saw the person, only a hand that pushed a lighted coal oil lamp with a wick and tall chimney. The light showed the first man plainly. Half of his spine had been blasted out by the buckshot. He wasn't moving.

The second man sat against the door jamb. His chest was a mass of blood. His head lifted.

"Help me!" he pleaded.

Both were no longer dangerous. Colt grabbed the lamp and stepped around the two dead and dying and pushed the light around the door. He bent and looked into the back yard from floor level.

What he saw let him relax. The man in the

back yard had lost most of his face and half of his head.

Colt brought the lamp back to the wood-shed and set it down where he could see the man against the door. He was chopped up too much to be alive.

Colt touched the man's face. There was still a pulse.

"Who hired you? Who sent you here?" Colt asked. The man's eyes came open for a fraction of a second. "Hired us? Saterlee. To kill Overbay."

"You swear?" Colt asked.

Sergeant Dunwoody and a private knelt beside Colt.

"Who hired you to kill Mr. Overbay?"

"Indian Agent Saterlee hired us three to gun Overbay. Now help me!"

The desperation in the man's voice chilled Colt a moment. Then the bush-whacker's head rolled to one side and a last spasm of movement came through his body and there was a rush of air out of his lungs.

"Sergeant Dunwoody. Go find the Town Marshal. He'll have to make out a report."

J. A. Overbay came into the woodshed. He was trembling.

"Mr. Overbay, come look at these men and see if you recognize any of them."

The merchant shook his head. "Drifters

probably. Any time of the week you can find half a dozen in some of the saloons in town." He blinked back tears. "Colonel, I don't know how . . ."

That was as far as he could get. He shook so hard he couldn't stand up. He melted to the floor and lay there trembling.

"Help him get to the front room couch," Colt told two of his men. Then he leaned back against the woodshed wall and waited for the lawman to arrive.

There would be forms to fill out. Whenever a civilian died there were always forms.

Ten miles from Prairie City, at just after 9 o'clock the same evening, Mike Guthrie was reading a bedtime story to his five year old daughter in her upstairs room when a dozen rifle rounds slammed through the lamp-lit windows of the ranch house.

He dove for the floor, pulling the little girl with him. He dragged down a blanket, wrapped her in it and pushed her under the bed.

"Stay there!" he shouted, then ran down the steps and dove to the floor as more rifle rounds broke out the front windows.

He had taken the warning from the army man seriously. None of his riders were in the bunkhouse, although the lamps were lit. His wife was safe in the root cellar with his two small sons. But Janie, his little girl, was afraid to be in the root cellar.

Now he crawled to the dining room table and lifted down the twin lamps there. He blew them out. Two more hands in other rooms did the same thing. He had fifteen men mounted and clustered in hard to reach positions within a quarter of a mile of the ranch.

He hoped that if the attackers came, they would miss his outriders and then be ringed in. It might have worked.

"Don't fire unless you have a target," Guthrie called. "We don't want them to know how many of us are here."

Guthrie was back by the open front door. He had nailed the screen door open earlier. Now he saw a pinpoint of a flickering flame maybe thirty yards away. His rifle came to his shoulder and he fired twice around the flame. He heard a scream and the fire died on the ground.

"Watch for flaming arrows," he bellowed.

Guthrie heard a pair of rounds slam away on the back side of the house, then all was quiet.

Guthrie had instructed his outside men to wait for gunfire, then to ride in slowly toward the house watching for anything that moved.

He heard a rifle shot somewhere away from the buildings, then another one.

All was quiet for a while, then Guthrie saw someone running toward the bunkhouse with a flaming torch. Six shots bored through the night air toward the fire man. But he had thrown the torch before he went down. The roof of the bunkhouse blazed up and the gunmen could see the injured Indian crawling away. Two rifle rounds ended his crawl in a bellowing scream of anguish.

All was quiet for a few minutes. Then a flaming arrow flashed through the already broken front window.

Guthrie lifted up from the floor with a heavy blanket and ran to smother the flames before they got a chance to spread. As he ran toward the fire, six rounds from the attacker's rifles plowed through the broken windows at the light of the burning arrow.

"Oh damn!" Guthrie shouted. Something had blasted into his shoulder, spinning him around. He drove on forward with the blanket, kept low under the level of the window and fell on the flames which were starting to burn into a braided rug. He pounded them with his fist through the blanket until they stopped smoking.

"You hurt bad, Mr. Guthrie?" his ramrod called.

"Hell no! Now get the rest of those bastards. Probably all Indians from the damn reservation."

The outriders now moved closer to the buildings. Guthrie heard a flurry of gunfire behind the barn, then another past the corral.

He crawled to the hall and found where his wife kept the sheets. He ripped one into pieces and tried to tie up his shoulder. He bled like a stuck shoat.

Eldridge, his ramrod, crawled over, lit two matches in the hallway where they couldn't be seen outside.

"Not too bad, boss. You'll live. Let me do a few turns with some bandages." He did. "Should top the juice running out of you."

The Guthrie men went back to their assigned positions. The bunkhouse still burned brightly, lighting up the side of the house and the barn. Guthrie could see none of his men and no Indians in those areas.

An hour later they had heard no new firing from any quarter. Mike Guthrie crawled halfway out the front door. He held his six-gun in front of him. The burned out bunkhouse gave off almost no light now.

"Hamilton! Dewey! You see anything else out there?"

Even as he said the last word, Mike Guthrie sensed movement just at the edge of the steps six feet away. Mike triggered the six-gun five times as he rolled to one side. Only one shot came from the edge of the front steps.

Nothing moved.

Not a sound could be heard by Mike Guthrie except his own racing heart and his gasping for breath. He had not been hit by the bullet.

"Hold your positions!" Guthrie yelled a few moments later when he felt sure of his voice.

A soft groan came from the steps.

Guthrie called for an unlit lamp to be passed up to him. He struck a match just inside the front door against the wall and lit the lamp, then pushed down the glass chimney. He stood beside the front door jamb and held the lamp.

He knew that just in front of the front steps was a bare place where some of the children played ranching. He held the lamp by its base and in one swift motion tossed it out the front door, over the steps so it would hit the hard dirt.

It did and the glass lamp shattered, igniting the coal oil on the bare ground and in the edge of some sparse grass.

He waited a moment, then shouted around the door.

"Anybody see anything near the front steps?"

"Hell yes, boss. A damn Injun there with two rounds through his chest."

"Tell me if he moves," Guthrie called. "We'll wait them out."

The men of the Guthrie Ranch were still in their same positions when the sun poked up over the eastern horizon the next morning.

Guthrie had not fallen asleep. He could count every second of every minute all night. The first thing he did was rush upstairs and look at his little girl. She lay where he had left her, still sleeping soundly. He lifted her out from under the bed and lay her on the mattress and covered her.

Then he went and brought his wife and two small sons from the root cellar.

He walked to the back door and rang the dinner bell. Mike Guthrie watched as his men came up from hiding places all over the yard and around the barn. Three men rode in on horses. They reported that they heard a half dozen horses riding hard before midnight and tried to follow them, but the riders got away in the darkness.

"No sense tracking them, we know where

they came from," Guthrie said. "Anybody make a casualty count? I got winged, anybody else hurt?"

Two men had minor gunshot wounds. One man broke his arm as he dove for cover.

"We killed three of the bastards," a cowboy said. "Leastwise we got three bodies out there that ain't moving."

"Load them on a wagon," Guthrie said. "Me and Joe with his broken arm, and them three dead Comanches. We going in and have another talk with the army, then we'll go see the doctor."

Emma Guthrie came out of the kitchen with a plate in her hand. "Nobody is leaving before they've had a good breakfast." Then she grinned. "That don't mean them three Comanches out there."

Everyone had a good laugh. It was the first in many hours around the Guthrie ranch.

11

Slade Rogers gripped both sides of his head with his hands. He wanted to pound his face against the wall until the pain went away. Sometimes he wanted to shoot himself so the agony would stop for all time. He tipped the pint bottle of whiskey and took a long pull at it.

Did it help? He couldn't tell. Not until he was drunk. Then he didn't feel the terrible brain-searing pain. He shivered and for a moment the pain vanished. Then he blinked and knew what he had to do. The damn Indians killed his family. All Indians must die! It was night, he wasn't sure what time. But it was dark and he could do it in the dark.

He left the room in the rear of the hardware store and slipped outside. He had his horse down at the livery. Ralph let him keep her there free. He cleaned out stalls on Sunday to pay Ralph back a little.

An hour and a half later, Slade slid into the brush along the creek that wound through the Comanche–Kiowa reservation. He had been here many times. Now the Indians seemed to be farther into the preserve.

Some seemed wary now, afraid of some unseen killer who struck in the night.

The bastards should be afraid! After what they did to his family! He would even up the score a little more tonight. Blood for blood!

Slade left his horse in the place he usually did. It was over a small rise from the stream and away from any of the tipis of either tribe. He moved forward slowly, sure that there would be some tipis along this gentle stream.

Horses. He heard horses rushing back into the reservation. He parted some brush and looked out on the rolling plains. Six horses charged through the faint moonlight. So late? They must be coming back from a raid. They probably had killed more wives and innocent children!

The six riders stopped a moment and talked, then they went their separate ways. The one closest to Slade seemed to be hurt. He carried one arm at his side as he rode fifty yards down a trail and stopped at a large tipi. He vanished inside a moment, then came out and walked to a nearby tipi and went inside.

Slade watched. He knew from many trips to the reservation that a little patience paid off. Ten minutes later an Indian came out of the closest tipi pushing someone ahead of him. Slade saw that the person was a woman, and he was sure it was a white woman! She went off a short ways and relieved herself, then the brave caught her arm and pulled her back inside the tipi.

He should remember something about a captured white woman, but for the moment he couldn't. The pains came back. He had to get rid of the pain!

Slade slipped up on the tipi where he had seen the brave and the white woman enter. He checked around the silent, dark woods along the small creek but saw no one. Then he lifted the flap of the tipi and slipped inside.

The soft glow of a fire lighted the area. An Indian brave heard the slight noise and lifted up from his low bed. Slade had out his eight inch skinning knife and he lunged forward ramming the thin blade deep into the Indian's chest, slashing through the top half of his heart.

The brave sank to the floor, gurgled as blood gushed into his mouth and fell over backwards, dead.

Slade looked around. The white woman sat up on another low bed. Slade rushed to her, took her hand.

"I'm here to help you," he whispered. He

must save her. He didn't know why but he must help this woman. They slipped out the flap and ran into the brush and toward his horse.

Two minutes later a scream billowed through the camp. Short Knife had returned from having his arm bandaged and found his friend dead and his captive white woman gone.

His screams brought a dozen warriors from their tipis, guns or bows in hand. Quickly he told them what had happened. He sent four warriors to mount their horses and ride along the nearest edge of the reservation so no one could escape.

He took the rest of the men and they fanned out in a long line and moved toward the north, toward the closest point to the edge of the reserve. Anyone rescuing the white woman would take her in that direction.

Short Knife moved through the brush and then the open space with speed and caution. He made not a sound. His rifle and the pistol in his gunbelt were ready.

Two defeats in one day were too much for him. The raid on the ranch had been a disaster. He and nine men had charged the place, only to be met by twenty guns, men hidden and waiting for them. They had only burned down one small building.

Three of his brave warriors had died on the raid. And it had accomplished nothing.

The owner, Guthrie, had not been killed as Saterlee wanted. Now the Agent would be angry with him. He would not lose his white woman captive the same night. He could not and keep his standing as the war chief of the Comanche in this camp if bad things continued to happen. The warriors would say his magic was gone.

"Go! Go! Find the white woman and kill whoever stole her. She is still my property, but I will reward the one who captures her."

Word spread quickly through the camp, even though it was well past midnight. Warriors, young boys and even some women began to prowl the reservation looking for the white-eye woman.

Well ahead of the first hunters, Slade held the woman's hand as they ran through brush, then across an open stretch of prairie to another brush line along a feeder stream.

"My horse is just ahead," Slade whispered to the woman. She nodded. "We'll get to the horse and you can ride behind me as we gallop back to town."

"But won't the Indians have horses as well?"

"They won't be able to find us in the dark."

As Slade came toward the last small rise behind which he had hidden his mount, he saw two Indian braves run from some brush and come toward them.

"Oh, dear!" Charlotte whispered in near panic. "What can we do now?"

He held his finger to his lips and urged her down behind a log. "Stay here," he said softly.

Charlotte saw him pull out a long thin knife and turn his pistol so he could use it like a club. Slade crawled a dozen feet and lifted up behind a cottonwood tree that would hide him from the approaching warriors. One of the Comanches carried a rifle, the other a bow and arrow.

Slade held his breath as he listened for the Indians to come. He saw that they were angled almost directly for the tree. He hoped they kept the same course.

He hefted the six-gun. It would make a good club. For a moment Slade waited for the drilling, terrible pain to burn through his brain, but now he realized that it was not there. Only his heartbeat hammered in his ears as he waited. A stick broke somewhere ahead of the tree.

Slade pressed his back against it. The red

men would be on the left side of the tree. He put his knife in that hand and the six-gun club in the other.

A whispered few words came to him. The Indians were talking. Then they came forward. He saw a foot placed carefully on the woodsy floor. It tensed as if the body were swinging forward.

Slade darted out from the tree, the blade held in front of him like a lance. He was almost on top of the closest man. The blade drove into the Indian's side just below his rib cage. With a reflex action, Slade turned the blade and sliced it out through the Comanche's belly, as he lifted the six-gun and slammed it down hard on the forehead of the second Indian.

The first man fell away to the left, the second dropped from the vicious blow. It didn't cave in his skull but dazed him and he fell to his knees.

Slade saw him going down, jumped to one side and swung his boot forward in a powerful kick. The hard toe of his boot struck under the Comanche's chin and jolted his head upward so sharply that it broke his neck. The dying redman slumped to the right. Slade bent, grabbed the rifle and the small buckskin bag of shells the Indian had carried.

He ran back where he had left Charlotte, motioned to her, caught her hand and helped her stand. Then they ran forward up the slight rise to where he had left his horse.

The animal wasn't there.

Slade looked around in anger for a moment. Then he calmed. There was no headache. It always lasted until he got back toward town. Now it was gone. He didn't question it. He could think clearer.

The woman, Charlotte Albers, was the one kidnapped from the hotel. He had to save her and himself. But how, with half the Comanche nation hunting him?

First find his horse. Was this the right little hill? He looked it over critically. No. There had been two smaller cottonwoods spaced like sentinels. Which way? He chose the direction on his left which was slightly downhill here.

They ran again.

Charlotte looked at the wild man who held her hand. He was the same one who saved her that afternoon from that bully on the street. Slade Rogers from the hardware store. Yes, she remembered now, his family had been slaughtered by Indians about a year ago.

She struggled to keep up as he ran. He had been so gentle with her that afternoon.

Was that just the day before? The past twenty-four hours had been terrible. She had been treated like an animal, a *property*.

When Slade burst into the tipi she had been ready to try anything to escape. The sexual activity had not bothered her. The way Short Knife had treated her made her feel like a dog in heat. That had surprised and hurt her.

She crouched down beside a fallen log near the small stream because Slade did so. He put his finger to his lips and pointed ahead. She saw a horse nibbling on a few grassy shoots.

Slade checked the rifle. There was a cartridge in the chamber. He whispered for Charlotte to remain where she was and he made a quiet, quick circle around his horse. He found no traps, no problems. He caught the animal's reins and led it to the woman. He mounted and then hoisted her on board. She was heavier than he expected. She put her arms around his chest and they began to move slowly through the brush to the north. That had to be the closest edge of the reservation.

They rode for five minutes.

A rifle barked its deadly message, but the sound came from a half mile away.

"Don't worry, they aren't shooting at us,"

he said. It was the first time he had spoken in his normal voice since they left the tipi.

"While I'm with you I won't worry," Charlotte said. "I trust you. You saved my life back there."

"Maybe. We aren't out of here yet."

He stopped the horse and held up his hand, palm outward. The only sound Charlotte could hear were crickets and now and then an owl hooting a greeting to a mate.

Ahead, an Indian war pony nosed its way through some brush and came into the stretch of open prairie. The animal was less than a hundred feet away. Slade reached down and held his mount's muzzle closed with his hands. He didn't want his beast making horse talk with the other critter. The rest of the horse was now visible, showing a Comanche brave holding a rifle. He scanned the scene, passed over the shadow that Slade and his passenger made near heavier shadows of trees. He checked the landscape again, then rode slowly to the west and out of sight in the scattering of brush.

"You could have killed him," Charlotte said matter-of-factly.

"Yes. But it would have brought twenty more down on us."

"But didn't you come into the reservation to kill Indians? To kill them because they killed your wife and children?"

Slade watched her a moment over his shoulder. "Yes. But that's all over now. I don't need to see their blood anymore."

"That's good. Now how do we get out of here?"

"There's a trail near here."

"But won't they be watching the trail, hoping you'd try to get out that way?"

"Yes." He grinned. "You'd make a good soldier. We'll go north again, but a quarter of a mile over from the trail."

They rode. Fifteen minutes later after walking the animal the whole way, they saw the edge of the reservation ahead. It was marked by a low bluff that ran for miles through the country here.

"Just past that small bluff and we're out of the Indian country," Slade said.

Before Charlotte could reply a Comanche battle cry daggered through the night air and two horsemen rode hard at them from directly ahead. Slade stopped the horse, lifted the rifle and fired. One of the Indians spun off his mount with a bullet through his heart.

The second Comanche swung off the side of his horse. Slade calmly reloaded the single shot rifle and fired again, this time hitting the horse in the head and tumbling him down in a fury of long legs and heavy body crashing to the ground and rolling three times. The Indian brave who spilled in the fall failed to get up.

Slade kicked his mount in the flanks.

"Hang on!" he shouted. "They'll be coming at us from all over now."

He kicked the horse into a gallop and urged more speed from it. There was a risk, Slade knew, but a sudden obstacle or a gopher hole seemed like an unlikely problem now. If they didn't move quickly they could have their brains boiled out of their skulls by morning.

They raced through the grass, across a small draw, and headed up the other side just as three Indian horsemen started down. Slade jerked his mount to the side and galloped down the draw a hundred yards, then turned north again.

One of the three horsemen saw what he tried to do and rode parallel with him.

Slade fired his revolver at the rider, but missed. The Indian had a revolver of his own and jolted three hot chunks of lead at the double-mounted horse, but all missed.

Suddenly Slade skidded the horse to a stop, lifted the rifle and fired. The war pony went down. Slade spurred his horse forward, darted over the small ridge and raced along for the bluff. Now he could hear other horses pounding along the ground. Most were behind him.

He rounded a small clump of brush and saw two Indian horsemen ahead in the soft moonlight. One fired a rifle and they felt the lead whiz by close.

Slade fired in return, then spurred his mount to the left. Two more horsemen appeared there, but no weapons fired. Slade loaded and fired at the new pair, scattered them and pounded between the startled Indians. He charged up the bank and was out of the Indian zone.

"Don't make no never mind to them, they'll still be after us," Slade said. "They can catch us on this old nag."

They rode at a fast gallop for another quarter of a mile, then slowed and let the horse walk. She was almost winded. Slade patted her, rubbed her nose, massaged gently along the side of her sleek head.

"Used to have this horse with me at my farm. Fact is, she and I were the only survivors. I was out on her when the savages hit us."

"You can talk about it now," Charlotte said.

He brightened, turned and grinned. "Damned if I can't!"

"You know what else? There doesn't seem to be anybody chasing us. I think they turned back. I think you shot one of them back there. Maybe it was Short Knife, the one who kidnapped me."

"That would do it. Nobody to offer a reward anymore. He probably told them he'd pay five horses to the man who recaptured you for him."

"Five horses!"

"Hey, that's a goodly sum for a wife, even for a Comanche."

They both laughed.

Then they rode on toward Prairie City. Without pursuit there didn't seem to be so much rush.

A mile on she touched his shoulder.

"Mr. Rogers, could we stop for a minute? I need to . . . I mean all of this excitement. . . . Could we stop, please?"

He pulled up, helped her down and turned his back. "You just go ahead and pay Mother Nature a call. I'm watching for Comanches."

She came and tapped his shoulder a short time later. "Thank you, Mr. Rogers. That was good of you. I feel ever so much better."

"Ever so welcome, Mrs. Albers."

"Would you . . . could you call me Charlotte?"

"Only if you call me Slade."

"Done. Let's walk aways, give the horse a rest."

She stumbled and he reached out and took her hand. "Makes walking across here ever so much easier," he said.

"Thanks."

A quarter of a mile later they mounted the horse and rode along in silence.

"I been thinking of shaving off my beard and getting my hair cut," Slade said. "Think you would know me then?"

"I'd certainly like to try to see if I would."

"Done," he said. He looked at her. "Surely do wish you wasn't married, Charlotte."

"Why, Slade Rogers. What a strange thing to say."

"No, I mean it. Never thought about a woman once since my wife died. But now, with you out here, the danger and all. Well, I just reckon I could indeed appreciate a woman like you."

"Thank you, Slade. Nicest thing any man has said to me in . . . in years."

They let the horse walk along through the silence again.

"You know . . ." She stopped. "You've heard that I'm not very . . . faithful to my husband. Isn't much of a secret around town."

"I heard."

"I learned a lot this past day and a half. I figure if I had me one good man, one who could get it hard and do me right in bed, then I'd be content."

"Walt can't do it?"

"Not for two years."

"Damn!"

"Afraid I haven't handled it all too good."

"Damnation! Christ. No wonder. . . . could you get a divorce from him?"

"He offered when it first happened. I know he'd agree to a divorce. He said once he'd give me a divorce and twenty thousand dollars. I'm a real embarrassment for him."

Slade kicked the mount into a trot. "Charlotte, now I'm in a rush to get back to town. Gonna have me about three baths, and then a shave and a haircut. Before you say anything more I aim to get it up and show you I can do you good in bed. Then it's up to you. I mean, I guess I'm asking you to marry me."

12

Colt and his five tired men got back to the fort well after midnight and fell into their bunks. The next morning Colt badgered Colonel Mason into giving him twelve more men to use to guard Overbay's house and his business until the matter could be settled.

"Shouldn't take more than a day or two," Colt said. "We're close to nailing down the whole thing. This is legitimate Army business. We're guarding a witness in a federal prosecution."

The Fort Commander gave in after a small protest, and Colt selected the dozen men and sent them out with a corporal in charge of each detail.

"Guard these two structures and the owner," Colt instructed. "This is a 24-hour guard, so take enough field rations for two days and set up your own hours. I want at least three men on duty at each place around the clock."

The men grumbled some but marched away to a different kind of duty for a change.

Colt was in his quarters working up a bill of charges against Hirum Saterlee when

199

through the window he saw a wounded civilian race into the fort and up to the Commander's office.

Colt went to see what the problem was, along with a dozen other officers.

"Renegades, my guess," the man said. "I'm a rancher, about twelve miles out northwest. Twenty Indians hit us early this morning. Burned down my barn and my house. My wife and kids were here in town for some kind of a celebration. I was out on a roundup. I got back in time to get off a shot or two and get myself shot up. The heathens raced off toward the next ranch, Bajelland's place, about five miles farther out.

"Bastards killed three of my hands, scattered 300 head of steers I just rounded up. I want those bastards to pay for the murderers they are."

Colt had heard enough. He sent a runner for Sergeant Dunwoody with a message. "Have your five men ready to ride in fifteen minutes."

Colt called his orderly to bring his horse around field ready. He checked the Spencer rifle he had drawn and a dozen extra tubes loaded with ammunition. He went in to see the Colonel. "I need twenty men ready to ride in twenty minutes," Colt said. "We'll go after those renegades. We can get between them and the reservation and cut them off."

Colonel Mason didn't argue this time. He gave orders to his First Sergeant and a special field unit was ready to ride in a half hour with two days of rations.

Colt led his 26 men out past the flagpole and turned them northwest. The rancher who had come in bloody and on a worn out horse went with them as guide. He had been patched up and bandaged. The blood looked more serious than the wounds actually were. He rode a fresh army mount and carried an army Spencer.

"You know how to use that thing?" Colt asked, nodding at the weapon.

"Does winter bring the snow? Hell yes, I can use one. Wait until we get within range, I'll show you."

"You said they were heading for the next ranch north of yours. Why didn't they just rustle your livestock and head back to the reservation?"

"What I been asking myself. They seemed more interested in burning and wrecking things. One Injun had a bandaged up left arm. He seemed to be running things. He is pure hell on a war pony, I'll say that for him."

Colt lifted the pace up to a canter and watched the men. Most adapted to the jolting ride, but he quickly saw that the horses responded to it. The horses moved well at that pace and it was natural for them. Colt had run a horse for eight hours that way and it wasn't even lathered up.

He figured an hour and a half to make the first ranch. They did it in five minutes less than that.

The rancher said his name was Ned Lincoln. He left instructions with his ranch hands and then joined the troopers bringing one of his men along.

"Best shot in the state," Ned said to the new man.

"How far to the next ranch?"

"Five miles. We better bear a little more east now, follow that rise of land."

They saw the smoke from a mile away.

"Barn is gone," Ned said. "They probably hit it first. They'll loot the ranch house. Maybe we'll get there in time to save it."

When they were half a mile out on the gentle downslope, Colt ordered the men to each fire one rifle round in the direction of the ranch.

"We'll let them know we're coming," Colt said grimly. "We might help save somebody."

Colt could see riders around the ranch buildings still standing. When his men fired, the activity increased.

Colt brought up Sergeant Dunwoody. "Take half the men and cut due east. We'll try to cut them off from running around our flank. Go now."

Dunwoody saluted and cut off the last three ranks of the column of fours and charged east.

"Bastards!" Ned growled as they rode.

When they were three hundred yards away, Colt sent his men into a company front, spreading out his thirteen men in one charging line with five yards between men.

Half a dozen figures mounted war ponies and raced out of the ranch yard. The house hadn't been set on fire yet.

"Fire at will!" Colt bellowed and rifles cracked. Colt was in the middle of the line. His men charged forward, sweeping the last ten hostiles from the farm yard. He saw two bodies on the ground, but charged past.

He levered a new round in his Spencer and came down on his target, a hard-riding Comanche ahead of his forty yards. The round sped out of his Spencer and smashed into the back of the rider, crushing his spinal column and pitching him dead into the

Kansas soil as his horse whirled and raced south.

Colt held up a moment and watched the flight of the savages. They raced away to the east, but turned south. Good, directly into Dunwoody's path.

"Chase them!" Colt bellowed into the prairie sky. "Drive them into Dunwoody's force."

They rode hard for ten minutes, and saw the Indians ahead of them slow and then whirl, driving to the east again. The rifle fire came clearly then as Dunwoody's force shot from horses standing still, greatly improving the troopers' accuracy. Three of the Indians went down in the gunfire. Two more turned and raced to the west.

Colt and his half of the force closed quickly, firing as they charged forward. Now there were only eight savages on horseback. Dunwoody's men rode hard again, taking an angle across the prairie to choke off the escape.

Colt drove forward sealing up the north route and turning back south the three hostiles who tried to slip past them.

Twenty minutes later the small drama was set. Dunwoody and his twelve men blocked any escape to the south. Colt had placed his men in an arc around the six

Indians, who had taken cover in a small draw where spring rains had gouged a runoff ditch six feet wide and three feet deep.

They had tied their war ponies to some shrubs fifty feet away. Now they lay in the protection of the Kansas earth and challenged the white-eyes to come get them.

"This is a lot different than the usual Indian fight, corporal," Colt said to the trooper to his right. "Usually the Indians have a half dozen of us pinned down in some godforsaken wash somewhere." Colt had brought his men to ground and worked up to within fifty yards of the hostiles.

"Two men fire to keep their heads down and the third move up to the next bit of cover," Colt ordered.

The men looked at the few dips and hollows that could provide any protection.

Colt looked at the man beside him. "You and you," he indicated the next man. "Give me three spaced rounds each at the very top of that gully down there. Now!"

Colt pushed his feet under him and the moment the first shot slammed into the ravine, he lunged forward, dug his boots into the Kansas soil and raced ten yards forward to a dip in the plains where he skidded to a stop. He made sure the muzzle of his

Spencer carbine was clear, then sent two shots at the ravine. He had an angle on one of the Indians.

Colt sighted in carefully and fired. He heard a bellow of pain as the round slammed into the calf of one of the red men.

Colt looked back and nodded and two more men fired and this time two sprinted forward. Colt added his rounds to the covering fire.

One of the warriors came crawling down the ravine toward Colt, who let him come until he was fully exposed. Colt sighted in on the man's chest, then called out. The warrior looked up, an expression of surprise and terror on his face as Colt sent the big .52 caliber Spencer round smashing into his chest, rolling him over on his back. He never moved again.

An hour later Colt saw that they could drive no farther forward. One of his men had been hit in the leg as he tried to get the next surge forward. There simply was no more cover. They were stalled.

Colt felt the wind. It was with him, but there wasn't enough to help much. A range fire? He considered it again, then decided to try it. If nothing else it would provide a smoke screen for him and his men to charge forward.

He took out matches and struck three, holding them together, then pressing them into a clump of dry grass. It caught at once and blazed up, but quickly burned out. Colt edged around in his cover to the far side of the small hump. There the grass was thicker and drier.

He tried again. This time the flames spread and caught hold and in two minutes it had spread to a thirty foot wide wall of fire and smoke that crawled slowly ahead toward the ravine.

"Fire!" one of the troopers yelled.

"Right," Colt answered. "In about thirty seconds we charge forward right behind the fire and the smoke. The hostiles won't be able to see us until we're on top of them. Get ready. Don't fire or make a sound until we're right on top of them."

Colt heard the men passing the word down the line. The fire burned brightly for a moment, sending up a heavy cloud of gray smoke that now blew forward over the ditch.

"Now!" Colt called.

He saw troopers lift up and start running forward. He charged ahead, then slanted to the left where he had seen the savages. Only one shot came from the coughing and eye-rubbing Comanches.

Colt's men overran them, blasting them with pistols at close range. Colt silenced one hostile who had a pistol of his own. Colt beat him to the trigger and the Comanche's head blasted backward and the top of his skull cracked open as the big round emerged.

Then the fire died out at the edge of the ravine, and Colt and his men checked the remains.

Colt had just left one dead Comanche when the Indian in front of him lifted up with a pistol. Colt kicked it out of his hand and smashed the butt of the Spencer alongside his head. The Indian lay there dazed but not dead.

"You'll be a general someday, colonel," the Comanche said.

"What?" Colt frowned. "You speak English?"

"As well as you, Colonel. It was a fine tactic squeezing us between your forces. That surprised me."

"You were the one at the alley who spoke English," Colt said.

"Yes. I am Short Knife."

"You've been the whole army for Hirum Saterlee?"

"A small army, but effective."

"Did you attack the freight wagon train?"

"Yes, that was simple. They didn't expect us."

"You killed them all on Saterlee's orders?"

"Yes, we couldn't allow any witnesses."

"Eleven men died that day."

"A thousand Comanche have died at the hands of the army. You do not weep for them."

"I am a soldier."

"I am a Comanche warrior."

"You're wounded."

"Three times. At the ranch last night."

"What ranch?"

"The Guthrie ranch. Saterlee wanted us to kill Guthrie. We couldn't, he was waiting for us."

"Hit bad?"

"Gut shot."

"You've got an hour."

The corporal came up and whispered to Colt that all of the other Indians were dead. Colt nodded and the man stepped away. Colt still didn't trust the Comanche.

Colt saw now the bandages on the Comanche's arm, and another on his leg. He could see no belly wound.

The colonel let his revolver lower. "I don't see your belly hit."

"You won't!" Short Knife screamed as he

pulled a derringer from under his leg, lifted it and fired all at once. Colt felt a sledgehammer blast against his right arm. It spun him half around. He whipped back with his .45 six-gun and triggered three rounds. Two hit Short Knife in the chest and one in the head.

The Indian never moved again.

"Corporal!" Colt called. "Get over here, I need you."

Ten minutes later Colt's right arm had been bandaged with a torn up shirt. A detail picked up all of the Comanche's weapons, bows and arrows, rifles and pistols.

Dunwoody came up with his blocking force. He had salvaged three enemy rifles, also according to army regulations.

Dunwoody stood and looked down at Short Knife.

"This is their general? He's the little bastard who has been causing us all the trouble?"

"That's him. Short Knife he said his name was. He spoke good English. He must have lived with a white family for several years when he was a kid."

"Too bad," Dunwoody said. "He could have been a real leader for his people, helped them learn to live on the reservation — learn a new way of life."

"Yeah, he had a chance at it but he failed.

Let's get the troops back to the fort. On the way back we'll stop at both the ranches and give them any help we can. We'll be riding into the fort late tonight."

"About as usual," Sergeant Dunwoody said and grinned.

"Oh, one more item. Get the Indian horses. Have Short Knife tied over his saddle. I want to send his horse back to the reservation so Saterlee will know that his enforcer, his army general, is out of the war."

Colt's arm began to get stiff before they left the second ranch. They had helped bury five people, rounded up some horses and set up a tent for the family to live in at Ned's ranch. Then they rode for the fort.

By the time Colt got to the fort physician, his arm was hurting so he could barely lift it. The derringer bullet was still in his arm and had to come out.

The army doctor put him on a wooden table with three lamps over it and held a small bottle.

"Colonel, we're going to try something new. I've used it two or three times. It's called sul-ether. I'll put some on a cloth over your nose and I want you to breathe deeply. After a few breaths you won't feel a thing, you'll be unconscious and I can do my work with no interference."

"Right now I don't care much if I wake up or not," Colt said.

"You will, believe me. I've used this before. Now relax and breathe deeply."

When Colt came back to reality the bullet was out of his arm, it was bandaged, and he lay on a cot. His arm didn't hurt as much. He mumbled something about his job not being through yet. "Still have to get Saterlee," he said, then he drifted off into a deep sleep.

13

Lieutenant Colonel Colt Harding had left orders the night before with Sergeant Dunwoody to have the same troopers he rode with that day assembled and ready to ride at six A.M. He had also told the doctor to wake him up from the hospital bed by five-thirty.

Colt mounted his horse using only his left hand. His right arm was in a sling the doctor insisted that he wear for the next three days. The 26 troops, minus the one who got wounded the previous day, rode up to the gate at the reservation slightly before seven A.M.

A lone sentry stood at the gate. He was unarmed, but when he saw Colt and the blueshirts, he took off running into the brush along a small stream.

"Give chase?" Sergeant Dunwoody asked.

"No, I'm sure Saterlee knows we're coming by now." But Colt picked up the pace and five minutes later they pulled up in front of the Indian Agency House.

Hirum Saterlee sat on the porch rocking in a big chair. He smoked a cigar and waved off three Comanches with rifles who stood near the porch. The Indian Agent had a newspaper in his lap.

"Well, the army is up and out early this morning. You're trespassing on Co-manche–Kiowa territory, you know."

"Not true. We are here to arrest a law breaker, a man charged with several felony counts including eleven murders."

Saterlee pushed the paper off his lap. He held a burning cigar in one hand and a length of dynamite fuse in the other.

"Know what this is, soldier boy?"

"Dynamite fuse."

"Right. And it runs into that wooden box filled with fifty sticks of powder. You make any move to get off those horses and I light the fuse and all of us go up in a huge ball of fire."

Colt laughed. "Saterlee, for a politician you're a terrible liar. First place you're too much of a coward to do anything that would harm yourself, let alone blow your body apart. Second, there probably isn't more than a stick or two of dynamite in that box. It looks like an old one to me."

Colt swung down from his horse.

"Go ahead, Saterlee, blow us all up. I'm waiting."

"Damned if I won't!" Saterlee screamed.

He pushed the burning cigar end against the fuse until it started sputtering and burning. Colt watched it. The fuse was eight feet long to the dynamite box.

"Saterlee, you aren't much on using dynamite. First thing to learn is that dynamite fuse burns a foot a minute. Take about six to eight minutes for it to burn all the way to the box."

Colt walked up, took out his knife and cut the dynamite fuse in half and held the burning three foot end.

"Timing is important when you use dynamite, Saterlee. Damn important." He threw the burning fuse back at Saterlee, who pushed it off his knees where it fell.

Colt kicked over the dynamite box. There was nothing inside it except the end of the dynamite fuse.

"Now, Saterlee, you have any more tricks before I arrest you for murder, fraud and theft?"

"You can't prove a thing."

"Short Knife confessed to everything last night before he died. Yes, he got one bullet in me, but my three dug through him in much more deadly areas."

Saterlee lifted a sawed off shotgun from beside the rocker. "I'm not going anywhere, soldier boy. You ride back to your little fort and play your soldier games."

Colt shook his head. "And they told me you were smart, that you'd have all sorts of tricks. So far both of your moves have been shitass dumb. That thing's only got one barrel. How fast you think you can reload after you put me down? As soon as that thing went off, you'd have twenty rounds in your body. Is that what you want? I figured you were not totally brain-dead dumb."

"I'm not dumb, soldier boy. Look behind your men. This was just a little diversion so my troops could get in place."

Colt turned and looked behind his mounted men. He saw a half circle of more than a hundred Indian warriors, all armed with rifles, pistols or bows and arrows.

Saterlee stood now still holding the shotgun. "You soldiers on horses, you have thirty seconds to drop your rifles and revolvers on the ground. Then you will ride off the reservation in an orderly manner with the sergeant in charge. The Comanche have asked to have the colonel be guest of honor at a small bonfire meeting they're going to have."

"Hold your weapons, men!" Colt barked at them. "I figured I might need a second force to back me up. Tell your Indian friends to look over by the trail to town."

As Colt said it an artillery rig rolled up, the two horses swung around in a tight turn so the shooting end of the canon aimed toward the Comanches. Two men jumped forward and took the cover off the weapon. It was a Gatling gun. The thirteen barrel weapon sent a stream of bullets over the heads of the savages. Half of them fell to the ground. Twenty turned and ran into the brush by the stream.

"Hold your fire!" Colt bellowed.

The Gatling gun stopped firing. Then the artillerymen turned the weapon and trained it on the remaining group of armed Indians.

Colt looked back at Saterlee, but the Agent wasn't there.

"He ran behind the house," Sergeant Dunwoody said.

Colt pointed to three men and they dismounted and followed the Colonel as he ran to the side of the house and looked around. The scattergun blasted out its load of bird shot and Colt jerked his head back behind the wood just in time.

"Now!" Colt barked and the four men surged around the corner and charged at the flustered Saterlee who was trying to reload the shotgun. He turned and darted behind a pair of Indian women who had come with baskets. He walked them away, staying in back of them.

"We want him alive," Colt said as the four men ran in pursuit. They came to a close by Indian village. There were twenty tipis along the small stream. They couldn't see Saterlee anywhere. Colt put the soldiers to searching the tipis as he watched the whole scene.

A minute or two later the village was shaken by a dynamite blast. Colt ran toward a small council fire area where he saw Saterlee sitting with a dozen small children standing around him, shielding him.

"I want you alive, Saterlee," Colt said.

"I'm not going with you." He ducked down a moment, came up and threw something. Colt saw the short fuse burning and ducked. The stick of dynamite hit the ground near two Indian women and exploded at once, blasting them to the ground where they wailed in surprise and from their wounds.

"I might not have known about dynamite before, but I'm a fast learner. I have a whole box full now and fifty three-inch fuses so they will explode in ten to twelve seconds. So back away with your men, or I start throwing at the women and children."

"Not even an asshole like you could do

218

that, Saterlee," Colt said.

Saterlee lifted up and threw another bomb. It hit the ground and rolled toward a young child sitting by the stream. The child, no more than two, saw the burning fuse and ran toward it. He had just reached down for the new toy when it went off. The child's mangled, lifeless body was blown a dozen feet away.

"Now believe me!" Saterlee thundered. "Take your troopers and get off the reservation, or I'll blow up half these children."

Colt motioned for his men to back away. They went back until they were in the brush and settled down out of sight.

"Give me your rifle," Colt snapped. The closest trooper handed him the Spencer.

"Sir, it fires a little high and to the right an inch or so at fifty yards."

Colt nodded and watched Saterlee. Now there was no chance he was going to stand trial. Saterlee had just killed again, in person this time, that tiny Indian boy. Colt sweat as he waited. Saterlee stood up a moment, then dropped down behind the children. He had to move sometime.

A young girl of fourteen or fifteen came across the camp. She saw Saterlee and ran toward him. He motioned her away but she continued forward, stepped through the shield of children who were so frightened that they would hardly move for her. When she was inside she said something to Saterlee. He laughed. Colt almost had a shot but the Agent bobbed down behind the children.

Colt watched with interest then as one by one the young children who had been shielding the Agent, slipped away. Five had left before he noticed. Saterlee screeched in anger at them and the others froze where they were.

The girl said something else and Saterlee turned and slapped her. Saterlee stood and Colt fired. The round shaved the heads of the tallest children but was slightly high and to the right of Saterlee's head.

A head shot was the only target he had over the screen.

Saterlee ducked low and then in rapid succession threw three of the short fused dynamite bombs around the camp. One blasted over a tipi, another blew apart a cooking fire and a third went off near two old women.

"Shoot again and I'll throw a dozen bombs!" Saterlee boomed. The older girl who had moved into the group stood and gathered up three of the smaller children in her arms and ran away from Saterlee with them.

He screeched at her. She let the children down and pushed them toward safety, then calmly walked back into the group. Saterlee slapped her again. The girl screamed, a high, wailing cry of anger and fury.

She lunged ahead, and then Saterlee was the one bellowing in pain.

The girl stood, threw something from the place and when it landed Colt saw it was the Indian Agent's cigar.

"He can't light any more fuses," Colt shouted. "Let's go!" He sprang forward along with the three troopers and they raced unopposed to the group of children.

The older girl urged the kids to go back to their mothers. She pushed some. They turned to look at the Indian Agent, who sat on the ground staring at the knife handle that extended from his fat belly. Blood flowed from the wound.

Saterlee's face was pale already from the lost blood. The Indian Girl shooed away all of the children, then turned to Colt.

"Me Bright Night," she said. "Saterlee no damn good."

Colt's serious face broke into a grin. "So you killed him," he said.

"Saterlee sonofbitch," the girl said. "No damn good. He kill my brother." She nodded at them, then went and picked up the shattered body of the two year old boy who had tried to play with the burning dynamite stick. She carried the body away.

Saterlee looked at Colt, who sat on the ground in front of him.

"Don't ask me for any help," Colt said.

Saterlee sighed. The knife in his gut moved and he screamed in pain.

"You're going to let me die? I'm a white man!"

"You're no man at all in my book. Where did you hide all the money you've stolen?"

"Go to hell, Colonel."

"Probably, but you'll be there within an hour." Colt stood and started to walk away.

"You going to leave me here?"

"Yes. I think some of the Indian women will want to have a word or two with you. They owe you quite a lot."

As Colt stepped back a young Indian woman with a knife stepped in front of Saterlee and screeched at him in her native tongue, then made a slice down his cheek with her knife. The woman whose tipi was ruined by the bomb ran up and grabbed one of Saterlee's hands and before he could react, she chopped off two of his fingers.

Colt turned and walked away. He wasn't sure he wanted to see any more of it.

Saterlee was a white man, even if he was a terrible one. Whatever happened to him he more than deserved. But Colt knew what angry Indian women could do to a man. His steps slowed, then he went on and pointed back toward the Agency house and his troopers followed him.

Just as they got to the woods they heard Saterlee scream again. The Indian Agent went on screaming as they walked away.

In the clearing around the Agency House, Colt saw that the troops had dispersed the Indian warriors and sent them away to their tipis. There had been an overwhelming show of firepower and the Indians had not really wanted a confrontation with a large force anyway.

"Next we find the money Saterlee must have hidden in the house somewhere," Colt said. "Let's have a look."

Sergeant Dunwoody came up and he and the original five troopers began searching the frame building. They found nothing.

Colt heard something at the door and looked up to find Bright Night standing there.

"Look for money?" she asked Colt.

"Yes. He must have hidden a lot around here somewhere."

Bright Night went to the end of the room,

moved a small rug and lifted up a section of the floor. She stepped back. Colt knelt there and lifted out a metal box nearly a foot square. Inside he found stacks of bills and gold coins.

He put the floor back in place.

"Thank you, Bright Night," Colt said.

"Saterlee no damn good," Bright Night said and ran out the door.

"While we waited we checked out that building over there," Sergeant Dunwoody said. "Place is stacked to the rafters with sacks of beans and salt and all sorts of dry food."

Colt thought about it a minute. He sent a trooper to report on the condition of Saterlee, then motioned to Sergeant Dunwoody.

"I'm appointing you as temporary Indian Agent for this area, Sergeant. That means you find the seven missing wagons somewhere on the reservation and bring them here. Parcel out the food as you think it should be done, but make sure these people have enough to eat. I'll send over those other three wagons we have at the fort. There should be someone from Washington out here soon. I'll leave our regular five troopers with you for now until you get further orders from Colonel Mason."

The trooper sent to watch Saterlee came back, his face white.

"Saterlee is dead, or soon will be. They cut him something terrible, just small slashes so he'd bleed. Then they stripped him. Now they have him strung up by his ankles on a tripod, and they can raise or lower him by a rope. His head is less than a foot away from a small fire they built. His hair has burned off. They're gonna fry his brains until his head explodes!"

"He who lives by fire shall die by fire," Colt said. "Sergeant Dunwoody, this place is all yours. That girl Bright Night probably can help you learn the ropes around here. Good luck."

Colt mounted using only his left hand, had the metal box handed up to him and he led the rest of the troopers to the fort. Colt thought of the Indian Agent toasting over the slow Comanche fire head down and decided to pass on noon mess call.

He wrote out a complete report to send through army mail to General Phil Sheridan. He detailed everything he could prove and told about the demise of the former Vice Presidential Candidate and Indian Agent, Hirum Saterlee.

From the metal box, he counted out over six thousand dollars. The money would be

225

kept in the fort safe until the new agent was appointed and then turned over to him for the use of the Agency.

Colt took a quick trip into town to see the banker. He explained the situation, and the banker showed the totals in the three Agency accounts. The official account had $37 in it. The private account of Hirum Saterlee held $2,347. A separate account set up in the name of the Saterlee Foundation had another $1,567. Colt said the U.S. Government was seizing the two private accounts and transferring the money into the Agency account, which would remain sealed until it was reopened by the new Indian Agent for the Comanche–Kiowas.

The banker started to protest saying he couldn't do that, but Colt indicated that the Bank itself might be found in collusion with Saterlee by opening the accounts with what had to be Government money. Banker Walter Albers soon agreed to the plan.

Colt walked down the block toward the Overbay General Store.

The shopkeeper saw him coming and met him halfway down the boardwalk.

"I need that complete list of all government goods you sold, Overbay. Do you have it ready?"

"I do. I figure I sold the goods for a little

over eighty-nine dollars. I only had the stuff for four or five days. This is a small town."

"An honest estimate?"

"Absolutely."

"Good. Give me a statement, and pay the money to the bank to be deposited in the Indian Agency account. Pay ten dollars a month for the next ten months and we'll call it square."

"Thank you. Most considerate."

"And after this, buy your goods legally. I'll have someone from the fort watching your receiving dock." Colt left with the man staring after him.

Just outside the store he saw a woman in a bright blue dress and no sunbonnet walking down the street toward him. She was beside a tall thin man, clean shaven and with no hat over his light brown hair. The woman was Charlotte Albers. She walked directly up to Colt.

"Colonel Harding, I want you to meet Slade Rogers. He rescued me from the Comanche. You don't recognize Slade because he got a haircut and a shave."

"Afternoon." He shook hands with Slade.

"Short Knife won't bother you anymore," Colt said. "He was killed in some fighting after he raided a ranch."

"Good!" Charlotte said. "Oh, did Walter

tell you? He's giving me a divorce and Slade and I are getting married and we're moving out West aways to open a hardware store like Slade always wanted to. Ain't that grand?"

Slade grinned and pulled Charlotte down the street.

Colt watched them go. Suddenly he was hungry for a good steak, or maybe liver and onions and bacon, and about a quart of new potatoes and little peas in a cheese sauce. . . .

He turned toward the hotel restaurant. He wasn't even thinking about his telegram to Phil Sheridan. He wasn't thinking about going home to see his family. That would come tomorrow. Right now he was hungry.

Colt slapped the trail dust off his blue pants and shirt and walked into the restaurant. Damn but he was hungry!

The employees of Thorndike Press hope you have enjoyed this Large Print book. All our Large Print titles are designed for easy reading, and all our books are made to last. Other Thorndike Press Large Print books are available at your library, through selected bookstores, or directly from the publishers.

For more information about titles, please call:

(800) 223-1244
  or
(800) 223-6121

To share your comments, please write:

Publisher
Thorndike Press
P.O. Box 159
Thorndike, Maine 04986